THE DEVIL'S CHILDREN

THE CHANGES TRILOGY
by Peter Dickinson

The Devil's Children

Heartsease

The Weathermonger

THE DEVIL'S CHILDREN

The Changes: Book One

by Peter Dickinson

DELACORTE PRESS / NEW YORK

Published by
Delacorte Press
1 Dag Hammarskjold Plaza
New York, New York   10017

Chapter decorations by Leo and Diane Dillon

MANUFACTURED IN THE UNITED STATES OF AMERICA

FIRST PRINTING

LIBRARY OF CONGRESS CATALOGING IN PUBLICATION DATA

Dickinson, Peter [date of birth].
The devil's children.

"The Changes—book 1."
Summary: After the mysterious Changes begin, twelve-year-old Nicola finds herself abandoned and wandering in an England where everyone has suddenly developed a horror and hatred of machines.
[1. Science fiction]   I. Title.
PZ7.D562De   1986   [Fic]   85-16178
ISBN 0-385-29449-2

for Rani Gagan Deep Singh

Five Weeks Before . . .

The tunnel is dark and clammy, raw earth crudely propped. Bent double under its low roof an elderly man jabs with his crowbar at the work-face, levers loose earth away, rests panting for several heartbeats and then jabs again. This time the crowbar strikes a hard surface just below the earth. He mutters and tries again, jabbing in different places, only to find each time the same smooth hardness blocking his path, sloping upward away from him. Wearily he fetches a camper's gas lamp and peers at the obstacle, picking loose earth away from it with shaking fingers, and muttering to himself all the time. Suddenly he bends closer, pursing his lips, and runs a torn thumbnail down a crack in the smooth surface. The crack goes straight as a ruler, and meets the edge of the slab at an exact right angle. It is not natural rock, but stone measured and cut by masons.

His heart, which a moment before had been thudding with exhaustion, is now thudding with excitement. But he is a tidy-minded man and works methodically to clear a whole slab, and then to find leverage under it for his crowbar. Several hours pass, but at last he settles the steel into a crevice and leans his weight on it. The stone groans as it lifts. The man has a pebble ready to wedge the slit open. As he steps back to rest from that first effort he knocks his lamp over. In the new dark he sees that the slit is glowing, with a pale faint light, like a watch-dial. Something else. He does not see it, but feels it. Beyond the stone slab a Power lies.

So The Changes begin.

On a fine June night the Cardiff express drummed below the dark hills. The moon had set and the stars were soft but strong. In the fourteen coaches passengers slumped half asleep, frowsting and prickly. In the cab the driver stared ahead as the green lights called him on from section to section; the rails glistened ahead like faint antennae probing into the soft wall of night. How could he know at what moment the nightmare began, when the details of the nightmare were exactly the same as those of the journey he'd made so often before? Only inside him the horror swelled and burst into a scream as he leaped from his seat. His hand came off the Dead Man's Handle, so the brakes cut in as the drive cut out. The deceleration slung him against the dialed control board, stunning him. He lay still on the cab floor while his train, untouched by the nightmare because it had no brain to infect, brought itself to a stop with its useless engine still drumming in the dark.

The shudders of braking startled the passengers awake. They stared around them. A man yelled and beat at the windows with bare fists. Before the train stopped they were running up and down the coaches, looking for a way of escape. By accident a man scrabbled a window open (the door latch was now a mystery) and they all fought each other to get through it, to drop into the dark, scramble up the embankment and run at random into the still fields.

On roads and motorways drivers forgot their skill and sat helpless while their cars or trucks hurtled off the tarmac. In factories the night shifts rioted and smashed. At Port Talbot a freak storm gathered and raged above the steel works until the lightning made the whole huge complex a destroying furnace. In ordinary houses, as dawn came on, the alarm clocks rang and sleepers woke to stare at the horrible thing clanging beside them. Some hands, out of sheer muscular habit, reached out for the lightswitch, only to snatch themselves back as though the touch of plastic stung like acid.

Day after day followed of panic and rumor. Cities began to burn, amid looting and riot. Then the main flights started, hundreds of thousands of people streaming away from their homes to look for food, safety, peace. It was no wonder that many families became split up; no wonder that in London, for instance, one particular girl decided that the best thing to do was to go back to her deserted house and wait for her mother and father to come and look for her. . . .

CONTENTS

THE DEVIL'S CHILDREN

Chapter 1

BECOMING A CANARY

"Nicola Gore," said Nicky. "I am Nicola Gore."

She turned on her right heel, kicking herself around and around with her left foot, until the leather of the heel began to drill a neat, satisfying hole among the roots of the six-inch grass.

"Nicola Gore," she said as she spun. "Nicola Gore. Nicola Gore. Nicola Gore."

She was talking to herself, of course, because there was no one else to talk to. The last living person she'd seen had been the one-legged old man who sat on his doorstep in the sun, waiting to die and talking about his boyhood in Hammersmith more than sixty years ago, when the noise of London traffic had been the rattle and grate of iron wheels on cobbles.

Now the only noise was birdsong, and Nicky saying her own name to herself, aloud in the enormous loneliness.

The old man had gone from his doorstep twelve days ago. She had promised not to try and look for him, because he had said his going would be the sign.

And it was nineteen days before that since she'd last talked to anyone she really knew, anyone who loved her. She turned and turned. It was taking longer to get dizzy now than it had when she'd first discovered the trick.

They weren't going to come and find her now, were they? She'd done what she'd always been told to, if ever she was lost—waited where she'd last seen Mummy and Daddy, waited for a day and a night and another day, watching the dull-eyed ranks of refugees straggle toward Dover. Then she had set her chin and walked the other way, back to the drained city, looking at all the faces of the people who were leaving but not answering any questions, no matter how kindly. If she went *home*, someone would come and look for her, surely.

But they hadn't.

Just in time, before the tears came, the long wave of dizziness began to wash over her. Nicky had discovered this trick quite early. If you could get yourself dizzy enough, you stopped being Nicola Gore, alone and frightened and miserable in great empty London, and you became a sort of daze without a name, a blurred bit of a blurred world. She went on turning as long as she could still stand. Then she fell.

When the blurs began to settle into shapes again they were the tops of trees. She lay on her back in the spider-peopled grass and looked at the blue, unmottled sky. It had been like that every day, except for the hideous thunderstorm on the road to Dover. Would it last forever? No, it was July now, but one day it would be winter. She'd have to go before then. She ought to go now, before she caught the sickness down the road, or another sickness from living on lemon soda and pretzels and nuts looted out of empty pubs. She must set her chin again, become hard and uncaring, endure a world of strangers.

She knew that when it came to leaving she would need something to *make* her do it, but the impulse to action levered her out of the grass. Listlessly she looked around the place which five weeks ago had been called Shepherd's Bush Green, London, W.14. A four-acre triangle of turf, crisscrossed with paths and dotted with trees; around it ran a wide road; blank shops lined the northern side, and unfinished towers of flats and offices rose to the south. Nasty engines squatted in the road, silent and useless; they were all dead, since the people who had once made them work and move had left, but even so Nicky preferred not to go near them. Luckily there were gaps between them, where Nicky could tip-toe through, then scamper along the pavement of Shepherd's Bush Road, around the corner and home.

That's where she ought to be now, waiting in case they came after all, but it was better here among the trees. This was where you could get furthest from the dead machines and the black unnatural roads that stank strangely under the downright sun. And she *had* pinned her notice to the door, saying where she was, just as she'd done for the last twenty-eight days. Still, perhaps she'd better go and see.

She turned listlessly on her heel again, knowing it was useless to go back home and that she would have to make the effort not to cry when she got there and found the notice untouched. Dully she kept turning, like a slow top, and felt her heel beginning to bite yet another neat round hole into the earth below the squashed grass.

About the ninth time she went around she saw a movement up at the east end of the Green.

At first she thought that it was just the dizziness, coming sooner than usual and making the world tilt about, but next time around she stopped being a top and stood swaying and peering. The movement was people.

For no reason she slid toward the nearest tree trunk and hid.

There were quite a lot of them, and the colors were

wrong. It was like a procession in fancy dress. All the
men had beards, and they wore mauve and pink and
purple hats. No, not hats. There was a word for them
. . . and there was a word for the women's bright, slim
dresses, which reached right down to their ankles . . .
and another word for these people with their strange
clothes and beards and brown skins . . . or was it all
something she had once dreamed she knew about?
There were blank bits in her mind nowadays. Perhaps it
was the loneliness.

Four of the men came in front, carrying heavy sticks;
behind them marched a big group pushing carts and
prams or carrying bright-colored bundles; several children walked among the prams; one cart was covered
with cushions, on which an old lady was propped up; at
the back came another four men, also armed with heavy
sticks. They moved very slowly, like a funeral, along the
north side of the Green. They were quite silent, apart
from the iron wheels of the handcarts grating on the
tarmac, until they were nearly opposite where Nicky
was hiding. Then a high voice shrieked an incomprehensible sentence from amid the group of prams and
the whole procession halted. They all began talking
together as they spread themselves out on the grass, sat
down and started to eat the food which the women
passed among them.

The dizziness had gone from Nicky's body but her
mind still seemed fuzzy with it. These people . . .

she'd seen men and women like them before, strolling along these very pavements, doing their weekend shopping . . . but that was in the part of her memories which nowadays she seemed to find it hard to think about, like dreams you know you've had but somehow can't bring back when you're awake. Now, staring at these dark-skinned, bright-dressed people, she only felt their difference and their strangeness.

But they were people, and they were going somewhere.

Her mind made itself up without being asked. She slipped away along the tree trunks, across the road at the gap between the bad machines, along the pavement to where the old traffic lights stood blind as stone, left down Shepherd's Bush Road—walking now, and panting with the heat, and her neck sore from where the collar of her filthy shirt stuck to the sweaty skin—and along her home street.

Not home anymore. The street was dead, and buzzing with flies in the stinking, tarry heat.

Yes, her note was pinned to the pink door, untouched; but this time she didn't feel her throat narrowing and her eyes peppery with useless tears. She pushed the door open and ran up the stairs to her own room. Even this, with its brown carpet and the pictures of ships on the walls, didn't feel like home now. She took her satchel from the shelf, wiped the dust off it with her sleeve, undid the straps and tilted the meaningless books out onto the floor. Into the bottom of the satchel she stuffed a jersey, a spare skirt, her party blouse, the socks she'd managed to wash in soda water, and her gym shoes.

Anything else which she needed or wanted? Not Teddy, comfort though he'd been. None of the school uniform. Nothing to make her remember home or Mummy or Daddy. That was all over now—it had happened to somebody else, a girl with parents to love her and look after her. But Nicola Gore was going to look after herself, and not let anybody love her again, ever. It wasn't worth the loss.

Out of her desk drawer she took the blunt hunting knife which she'd bought with her own money at the fair when she was staying with Granny at Hertford; and from the blue jar on the mantelpiece she took the coral and gold necklace which one of her godmothers had given her at her christening, but she could never remember which.

Then she ran down to the kitchen, picking her way to the larder between the horrible smashed machines. Two bottles of lemon soda and one of soda water from her last pub raid; the packets of nuts and the salty biscuits. Her satchel was full now, and heavy too. She slung its strap over her shoulder, picked up her pencil from the hall table, and pushed the door wide open until she could lean against it to write on her notice without its moving away.

She crossed out her last message, about being up at the Green, and wrote beneath it "I'm going away now. I waited for twenty-eight days."

She was pulling the door shut when she thought that that sounded as though she was blaming them, so she pushed it open again and wrote underneath "I'm sure you would have come if you could. Love, Nicky."

When she pulled the door shut for the last time she felt that there ought to be some way of fastening it, but she couldn't remember how the lock worked. So she just made certain that the drawing pins were firmly fastened into her note, turned away and walked down the street without once looking back. She started to be afraid that she would be too late, but it was awkward to run with her satchel so heavy. It didn't matter; they were still there when she reached the Green again; the strange, dark children were playing a game of "touch" under the trees.

Beyond them the adults lolled or squatted on the grass. The whole group chattered like roosting starlings. The noise of their talk bounced off the shop fronts, and all of a sudden made the green feel as though people were living there once again. Yes, thought Nicky, these foreign-looking folk would do. She could go with them, and yet stay strangers always. It was a good thing they were so different. She sidled like a hunter toward the scampering children.

She was waiting by a tree trunk, beyond the fringe of

the game, when one of the smaller boys scuttered from an exploding group which the "he" had raided. He came straight toward her squealing with laughter until he was hardly six feet away; and then he saw her. At once he stopped dead, called with a shrill new note, and pointed at her. Then he stood staring. His eyes were very dark; his hair was black and gathered into a little topknot behind his head. His skin looked smooth as silk and was a curious, pale brown—not the yellow-brown of suntan, but a grayer color, as if it was always like that. His mouth pouted.

The game stopped at his call, not quite at once, but in spasms of scuttering which stilled into the same dark stare. Now the adults' heads were turning too; the thick beards wagging round; the worried, triangular faces of the women turning toward Nicky. One of the women called; two children ran to her side and stared from there. The other children melted back toward the adults, looking over their shoulders once or twice. Several of the men were on their feet, grasping their heavy staves and peering not at her but up and down the Green. Now the whole group was standing, except for the little old woman who had ridden on the cart; she still sat on the ground and gazed with piercing fierceness at Nicky from among the legs of the men. Then she cried out suddenly, only three or four words, like the call of a bird. The words were not English.

A big man bent and scooped her off the grass, like a

mother picking up her baby; he carried her to the cushioned cart, which was brightly painted with swirling patterns—it was the sort of handcart that street-market stall holders had used for pushing their goods about. The old woman settled herself on the cushions, stared at Nicky again, and called another few words. At once the whole group trooped off the grass and took up their positions for the march.

Nicky ran forward from under the trees. They were all watching her still, as though she might be the bait in some unimaginable trap.

"Please," she called. "May I come with you?"

A rustle ran through the group like the rustle of dead leaves stirring under a finger of wind. One of the worried women said something, and three of the men answered her. Nicky could tell from their voices that they were disagreeing with her. The old woman spoke a single syllable, and the nearest man shook his head at Nicky. He was short and fat and his beard was flecked with gray; his hat was pink, only it wasn't a hat, of course —it was a long piece of cloth wound in and out of itself in clever folds to cover his head and hair.

"Please," she said again. "I'm all alone and I don't know where to go."

"Go away, little girl," said the fat man. "We can't help you. You are not one of us. We owe you nothing."

"Please," began Nicky, but the old woman called again and at once the whole group began to move.

They walked off quite slowly, not because they wanted to move like a funeral, but because they couldn't go faster than the slowest child. Nicky stood and watched them, all shriveled with despair at the thought of facing the huge loneliness of London once again.

She stepped into the road to watch the strange people turn the corner north. (If they'd wanted to go south they would have started down the other side of the Green.) But instead they went straight ahead, up the Uxbridge Road, toward the doorstep where the one-legged man had sat in the sun.

Nicky began to run.

Her satchel dragged her sideways and thudded unsteadily into her hip. A rat-tail of dirty fair hair twisted into her mouth and she spat it out. Her soles slapped on the hot pavement and the echo slapped back at her off the empty shops. When she crossed the big road at the end of the Green the strange people were only a hundred yards down it, so slow was their march. She ran on, gasping.

They must have heard her coming, because one of the four men who walked in the rear came striding back toward her, his stave grasped in both hands like a weapon.

"Go away, little girl," he said sharply. "We don't want you. We can't help you."

Nicky stopped. He was taller and younger than the fat

man who had spoken to her before, and frowned at her very fiercely.

"No! Don't go that way!" she said between gasps. "There's a bad sickness that way. An old man told me. He said he was going to catch the sickness and die. He made me promise not to go down there. He said he'd seen people staggering about and then falling down dead in the street."

The dark man moved his stave, so that it stopped being a weapon and became a stick to lean on.

"This is true?" he asked.

"Yes, of course."

He looked at her for several seconds, just as fiercely as before. Then, without another word to her, he turned and called after the procession in the strange language. Beyond him Nicky could see two or three faces turn. A cry came back, the man answered and another cry came. By this time the whole group had stopped.

"Come with me," said the man without looking around, and strode off up the street. Nicky followed.

Men, women and children stood staring and unsmiling, still as a grove of trees, while she walked between them. When they reached the cushioned cart where the old woman lay, the man stopped and spoke for some time. The old woman creaked a few words back at him. Her face was all shriveled into wrinkles and folds as though it had been soaked too long in water, but her thin hooky nose stood out of the wrinkles like the beak of a hawk, and her dark brown eyes shone with angry life. She looked like a queen witch.

"Tell your story again, please, miss," said the man.

Nicky had stopped panting, so she could fit her words together into proper sentences; but she was so afraid of the old woman that she found she could hardly speak above a whisper. She felt the other people drawing closer, so as to be able to hear.

"I used to bring food for an old man who sat on a doorstep," she said. "He only had one leg, which is why he hadn't gone away. He told me that quite a lot of people further down this road had stayed too, and now they'd got very sick and if you went near them you might catch their sickness. It was the sort of sickness you die of, he said. He said that they crawled out into the street, like rats coming into the open when they've eaten poison, but some of them danced and staggered about before they fell down. He made me promise not to go this way if he wasn't on his doorstep, because that would be the sign that the sickness had come up the street as far as where he lived. He wasn't here when I came to look for him twelve days ago, and he hasn't come back. That's where he used to sit, down there, opposite the church."

The group was still no longer, but wavering and rustling. Suddenly the starling clamor of voices broke out, all of them seeming to speak at the same time. The women drew their children close to them, and the men's hands began to gesture in several directions. A younger man with a very glossy beard spoke directly to Nicky, in English.

"Cholera, perhaps," he said. "Or plague."

He sounded interested, as though he'd have liked to explore further up the road and see which guess was right.

The big man who pushed the old woman's cart had pulled a red book from under the cushions and was peering at it amid the clamor; two of the other men, still arguing at the tops of their voices, craned over his shoulders. The old woman held up her arms suddenly and screeched like a wild animal, and the shouting stopped. She asked a short question, and was answered by a mild-faced young woman in a blue dress. The old woman nodded, pointed south, and spoke again. The crowd murmured agreement. The big man ran his finger down a page of the book, flipped over some more pages, and ran his finger on—he must be tracing a road on a map. Then the whole group picked up all they had been carrying; the pram pushers and cart pushers circled around; the old woman screeched and they all started back toward the Green. They filed around Nicky as though she were a rock in the road.

She stood, running her thumb back and forward under her satchel strap, and let them trail past. Nobody said a word, and only one or two of the smallest children stared. When the last four, the stave carriers, had gone she followed behind. One of them glanced over his shoulder and spoke to the man who had led her into the group. He glanced back too, said something, shrugged and walked on. Nicky trudged behind.

They turned right at the Green, south. Their pace was a dreary dawdle as they went down Shepherd's Bush Road, which Nicky had so often scampered along. Carefully she didn't look up the side street to where her note was pinned to the pink door, but studied instead a gang of scrawny cats which watched from a garden wall on the other side of the road; already they were as wild as squirrels.

Yes, she thought, I am right to go now. If I stay any longer I will become like those cats. She remembered how neat the strange children had seemed, even while they were playing their game of "touch," and wondered how she herself looked. You can't wash much in soda water.

At Hammersmith Broadway there had been either an accident or a battle, for two buses lay on their sides and a vegetable lorry had charged into the ruin, scattering crates of lettuce about. The wreckage stank and the procession edged well clear of it. A minute or two later they were on Hammersmith Bridge.

Here the whole group stopped and the adults broke into their cackle of many-voiced argument while the children crowded to the railings and gazed at the still and shining water. Small brown arms pointed at floating gulls or bits of waterlogged driftwood, ignoring the wrangle that raged behind them. Nicky wondered how they ever could decide anything if they were all allowed to speak at the same time. The big man found a sheet of paper under the cushions, a real map with many folds, and this was pored over until, once more, the harsh creak of the old woman decided the question. Mothers called their children to them; burdens were hefted; the march dawdled on.

They went so slowly that Nicky decided she could afford a few minutes more on the bridge; she would be able to catch them without hurrying. The river was beautiful, full from bank to bank as high tide began to ebb unhurriedly toward the sea. A sailing dinghy fidgeted around at its moorings as the water changed direction. Something about the river's calm and shining orderliness washed away all Nicky's resolution—the river ran to the sea, and over the sea lay France, and that's where Mummy and Daddy were, and a little boat like that couldn't be hard to sail. She could swim out to it and row it ashore, and then stock it up with pretzels and lemon soda and sail down the river, around the coast and over the Channel. And then it would be only a matter of finding them, among all the millions of strangers. They *must* have left a message, somewhere. Sailing would be nice—alone, but going to meet the people who were waiting for you, who would kiss you and not ask questions and show you the room they had kept ready for you . . .

Nicky's whole skeleton was shaken by a tearing shudder, like the jerk of nerves that sometimes shocks the body wide awake just as it is melting into sleep, only this shudder went on and on. Nicky knew it well. It had shaken her all that first nightmare morning, and once or twice since. It was a sign that somewhere a hellish machine was working.

She looked wildly about for a few seconds, not feeling how her mouth and lips were pulling themselves into a hard snarl like a dog's, nor how her legs were running down the street called Castelnau faster than they'd ever run when she'd asked them, nor how her hand was groping in her satchel for the hunting knife.

A bus towered in the road; the strange people crowded around it, chattering again. Nicky jostled between them and hurled herself at the young man who stood smiling beside the vile engine which churned its sick stink and noise into the air. Her knife was held for killing. The young man was the only person looking in her direction. He shouted before she was quite through the crowd, and started to back away around the bus. A hard thing rammed into her ear and cheekbone, jarring her head so that for an instant she could not see. In fact she could not remember falling, but now she was on her hands and knees groping dazedly for the dropped knife, not finding it, then crawling toward the drumming engine and feeling again in her satchel for a bottle to hit with.

The world seemed to be shouting. Tough hands gripped her arms and hoisted her up. She struggled toward the bus, but the hands held her, hard as rope. The young man was climbing again through the door of the bus. She lunged at the hands with her teeth, but the men who held her did so in such a way that she couldn't reach.

All at once the foul drumming stopped, and only the stink of it hung between the houses. A voice croaked an order. They all moved on, up Castelnau.

Slowly, like the panic of nightmare dying as you lie in the half-dark and work out that you really are in your own bed between safe walls, the lust of hatred ebbed. She felt her neck muscles unlock. Her hands and knees, where she had fallen, stung with sudden pain. She was so tired that she would have dropped but for the hands that gripped her. She let her head droop.

It might have been a signal for the others to stop, and for the clatter of arguing voices to break out again. Most of the voices were men's, but sometimes a woman joined in. At last something was settled.

"Are you all right now, miss?" said a man.

Nicky nodded.

"Why did you do that?" said the man.

"Do what?"

"Try to kill Kewal?"

"He made the thing go," she said. "He mustn't. I had
to stop him."

"Who told you to?"

"I don't know."

"Do you want to kill him now?"

Nicky looked around the dark, silent faces. The
young man she'd charged at stood directly before her,
smiling, his small teeth brilliant amid the gorgeous
beard. Only one of his eyes looked directly at her. The
other one squinted crazily over her right shoulder.
"No," she said.

"But if he tried to make the bus go again?" asked the
man.

"Yes," she said.

The hands let go of her and she swayed. An arm
curled round her shoulders to stop her falling—a woman's arm this time.

"You will come with us," said the man. It wasn't a
question. Now, at last, she looked up and saw that the
speaker was the big man who had been pushing the old
woman on the cart. A woman in a blue dress, the one
who'd answered the question about the sickness, knelt
down in the road and started to sponge Nicky's bleed-
ing knees.

"Yes," said the young man, Kewal, smiling and
squinting. "You will be our canary."

"Kaya?" said one of the women.

"When the miners go into the coal mines," explained

the young man importantly, "they take a canary with them; if there is firedamp about—that is carbon monoxide, you know—the bird feels it before the miners. Just so this girl . . . what is your name, miss?"

"Nicola Gore."

"Just so Miss Gore will be able to warn us of dangers which we cannot perceive."

"You are willing?" asked the big man.

"Most people call me Nicky," she explained.

"Good," he said, as if she had answered "Yes." She had in a way.

"Our names are easy too," said Kewal. "All the men are called Singh and all the women are called Kaur."

Several of the group laughed in a fashion that told Nicky that it was an old joke. A high, imperious voice croaked from the handcart.

"My grandmother does not speak English," explained Kewal as the big man turned and began a conversation in the strange language. The woman who had been dabbing at her knees rose and took her hand and started to clean the grazes.

"How is your head?" said a voice at her side. "I regret that I had to hit you so forcibly."

She turned and saw the fat man who had first spoken to her. He was smiling nervously. His eyes had the look of a dog's which thinks it may have done something bad but doesn't want you to think so.

"My uncle is very quick and strong," said Kewal. "Although he does not look it."

There was another little laugh among the group. Nicky felt her cheek.

"It's all right," she said. "It's still a bit sore but it's all right. It doesn't matter, Mr.—er—Singh?"

Her voice turned the last two words into a question. She knew that Kewal had been joking, but she didn't know what the joke was. However, the fat man smiled and nodded. The old voice creaked another order. You could hear it quite plainly through the chatter of the rest of the group.

"Come," said Kewal. "My grandmother wishes to speak to you."

The old woman was still just as terrifying as before. She lay on her elbow on the cushions and stared. She wore about five necklaces, and every finger of her left hand had at least two rings on it. Nicky wanted to propitiate her, to make her less fierce and strange, so without taking her eyes from the many-wrinkled face she began to grope in her satchel. The old woman spoke two sentences and the big man laughed.

"My mother is pleased with you," he said. "She says you fight well, like a Sikh. But now you must fight for us, and not against."

Nicky's fingers found what she wanted. She walked right up to the cart.

"Would you like this?" she said, giving a little half

curtsey: the old woman might be a witch, but she was a queen too. Nicky put the gold and coral necklace down on a blue satin cushion. The ringed claw picked it up and the bright eyes examined it, stone by stone. The old woman clucked, spoke again and put it down on the cushion.

"My mother is grateful," said the big man. "She says it is good gold and well-carved beads, but you must keep the necklace. You are to help us and we are to help you, so there is no need for an exchange of gifts. We will protect you, and share our food and drink with you. In return you will warn us if we seem to you to be embarking on anything which is dangerous or wrong. Things like Kewal starting the engine of that bus. Do you understand?"

Nicky tore her eyes at last from the old woman's.

"Yes, Mr. Singh," she said, more confidently this time.

The big man's lips moved into a smile under his dark-gray beard.

"You will have to learn our other names too, you know," he said. "Now we must march on. You will walk with my sister's family. Neena!"

Nicky picked the necklace off the blue cushion. She was glad she hadn't had to give it away.

Chapter 2

FIRST NIGHT

Neena, the big man's sister, was a dark little woman, only two or three inches taller than Nicky.

"You can put your satchel into my pram," she said. "I expect you're pretty tired."

She spoke so softly that Nicky could hardly hear her. She looked tired and worried herself. A sulky baby sat in the pram, almost hidden by a hill of bundles.

"Thank you," said Nicky, and propped the satchel on the handles of the pram, leaning it against the bundles. Then she found she was still holding the soda bottle which she'd taken out to fight with, so she unscrewed the top and started to drink. The lemon soda was nastily sweet and warm, and very fizzy with the shaking it had had, so that the froth bubbled back into her nose and made her sneeze; through her snortings she heard the boy in the pram begin a slow wail.

"Oh dear," said Nicky, "is that my fault?"

"He's thirsty," said Neena, "and we cannot spare much water because we have to boil it all."

She leaned her light weight against the handles to get the pram going as the rest of the group moved off. Nicky, walking beside her, felt in the satchel for another bottle and handed it to Neena. The baby was watching; its wail softened to a snivel.

"No," said Neena, "it's yours. You will need it."

"I can easily break into another pub," said Nicky. "That's how I got these."

Neena looked at her doubtfully for a moment.

"Thank you, Nicky," she said. "Push the pram please, Gopal."

A boy about Nicky's size took the handles and started to shove while Neena rummaged in her bundles for a mug; she filled it from the lemon soda bottle and tilted it carefully to the baby's lips. The baby put up a hand to steady it, but did not help much; still, Neena managed very cleverly despite having to glide beside the pram.

"My brother is nicer than this, really," said Gopal, "but he knows that something is wrong and that my mother is worried."

"Are you really all called Singh?" said Nicky in a half-whisper.

"Yes. It was an order of the guru three hundred years ago that all Sikhs are called Singh. It means 'lion,' and we are a soldier people."

He spoke very proudly and seriously.

"What are Sikhs?" said Nicky.

"We are Sikhs. My people are Indians—Indian Indians, of course, not American Indians—but many of us came to England, especially after the Hitler war. We have a different religion from you and from other Indians, and we carry five signs that we are different. Other Indians wear the turban, for instance, but we do not cut our hair or beards at all, ever; we carry a sword, to show we are soldiers; we wear a steel bracelet; we . . ."

"I can't see any swords," said Nicky, who had been puzzled by the explanation. She felt that she ought to know about the Hitler war, and about Indians, just as she ought to have known about turbans, but she'd forgotten. She was irritated by being forced to recognize another of those moments when she saw or heard something which felt as though she'd dreamed it before, but had forgotten the dream.

Gopal laughed and felt in the back of his turban. From it he produced a square wooden comb to which was fastened a toy scimitar two inches long.

"You can't wear a sword if you are working in a bank," he said, "or driving a train in the underground.

Not a real killing sword. So we wear our swords like this, but they are still a sign of our faith and a sign that we are a soldier people. We are a very proud race, you know. When a man joins the Sikh religion he becomes taller and stronger and braver. It has often happened. I've read it in my history books."

"How old are you?" said Nicky.

"Thirteen."

"I'm twelve. Shall I help you push the pram or are you too proud?"

He laughed again, as though he was used to being teased and didn't mind. His face was thin and his skin looked silky soft; he moved his brown eyes about a lot when he spoke or listened, in a way that was full of meanings. Nicky decided that she liked him, but that he was a bit girlish. It was only later that she found he was a true lion, worthy of his name.

"You can help me up the next hill," he said. "We'll give my mother a rest."

Neena—Mrs. Singh or Mrs. Kaur, Nicky decided she ought to call her—turned her weary face to smile at her son, then started to arrange the bundles on the pram so that the little boy could sleep.

In fact the next hill was a long time coming.

Castelnau is a flat mile from end to end, between friendly Victorian mansions; then it bends and becomes Ranelagh Gardens, quaintly ornate red houses with little unusable balconies crowding all down one side, and on the other a six-foot wooden fence screening Barn Elms Park from the street. Ranelagh Gardens twists to cross the miniature scrub desert of Barnes Common. Here a bedraggled horse stumbled out of the bushes and followed them, until one of the rear guard tried to catch it and it shied away.

On the far side of the common the road humps itself up over a railway. Nicky fulfilled her bargain by toiling beside Gopal to heave the pram up to the ridge of the hummock, but she could only just manage it, so much of her strength had the rage of her fight taken. On the bridge some of the children crowded to the wall and gossiped in English about the odd little station with its lacelike fringes of fretted wood, until angry voices called them back to the line of march. Down the far slope a pram ran away from its pusher and was caught amid excited shouts by the advance guard. It seemed to Nicky that the shouting and the excitement were much more than were needed for an ordinary pram trundling downhill with nobody in it, only bundles and cardboard boxes.

The long climb up Roehampton Lane was another matter. Ropes and straps were produced and tied to every cart and pram, so that two could pull and one could push. The men in the rear guard and advance guard had to do their share as well, but they pulled with one hand while the other held their thick staves ready over their shoulders. Neena returned to the handles of the pram and Nicky and Gopal each took a strap. It didn't seem hard work for the first few steps, but as the wide road curved endlessly upward Nicky began to stagger with weariness. Nobody spoke. The iron rims of the cartwheels crunched on the tarmac, and the eighty feet padded or scraped according to how they were shod. Nicky bent her head and hauled, seeing nothing but the backward-sliding road beneath her, hearing nothing but the thin whistle of her breath in her throat. She stumbled, and stumbled again.

As she was still reeling from the daze of her second stumble she heard the old woman's voice creak, and a man shouted "Ho, Kaka, you fat villain, give Miss Nicky a rest and work off some of your grease by pulling on a rope."

Nicky looked up hopefully. A roly-poly boy about eight years old came and held out his hand for the strap.

"Please," he said shyly.

"This is my cousin Kaka," said Gopal from the other side of the pram. "I have twenty-seven cousins, and Kaka is the worst."

Kaka smiled through his shyness as though Gopal had been paying him a compliment, and immediately gave such a sturdy tug at the strap that the pram shot sideways across the procession and Neena locked wheels with the pram next door. Even the weary women laughed as they scolded Kaka, and the men halted and leaned on their staves to watch the fun.

The march only stopped for a couple of minutes, but it felt like a proper rest. Nicky walked beside Gopal on the other side of the pram. It was interesting to see how warily the leading men looked into every driveway and side road as they went past, and how often the others glanced from side to side or looked over their shoulders, as though every garden of the whole blind and silent suburb might hide an ambush.

"Is everybody here your relation?" she said.

"No," said Gopal. "Daya Wanti—that's the old lady on the cart—is my grandmother, and she has four sons and two daughters. My mother's the youngest. All my uncles and aunts have married, and they have children. Some of the children are grown up, like my cousin Kewal and my cousin Punam, who washed your knees; and then my father has a sister who is married and has children, and there's a family who are relations of the lady who married my uncle Chacha Rahmta. He's the one who knocked you over."

"But everybody here is your relation or married one of your relations or something like that?"

"No, not quite. We have some friends who had come alone from India and decided to live near us. When the madness happened to all the English people, they gathered to us for safety. You don't mind me talking about the madness? That's what we call it."

"I expect so," said Nicky without thinking about it. "Is your grandmother the chief?"

"Oh no. The women have an equal voice with the men, and of course the voice of the older people is more respected than the voice of the younger people; but we all decide together what to do, and then . . ."

"And then my mother tells us what we are going to do despite that," interrupted a man from Nicky's other side. It was Uncle Chacha Rahmta, pulling steadily on a rope which was tied to a handcart laden with cardboard cartons. As he spoke, the old woman screeched from her cart and the whole party stopped as if she had been a sergeant major calling "Halt!"

"You see what I mean?" said Uncle Chacha Rahmta.

They had reached the ridge of the hill. Ahead the road dipped and curved into the small valley of Roehampton Village, and then rose almost at once toward Putney Heath and Wimbledon Common. But behind and below them were roof tiles, mile upon lifeless mile, spreading right across the Thames Valley and up the far northern hills. Perhaps a few hundred people were still living among those millions of rooms, eating what they could scavenge, like rats in a stable; otherwise it was barren as a desert, just long dunes of brick and cement and slate and asphalt. Far to the east something big was burning, where a huge ragged curve of smoke tilted under the mild wind.

The Sikhs broke into their clattering gossip even before they settled for their rest. The children were too tired now for running-about games, but pointed and badgered their elders about the cluster of high-rise flats which stood close to the road, like the broken pillars of some temple of the giants. The baby in the pram woke, and was lifted out to totter around on the pavement. The adults sat along a low wall, and passed bottles of water from hand to hand, from which each drank a few sips. Nicky felt thirsty again, but didn't dare start her last bottle for fear of making the baby cry. Perhaps if she moved further away . . .

Down in the dip, right in the middle of the village, was a pub. She stood up and trotted down the hill. A voice cried after her, but she waved her hand without looking around, to show that she knew what she was doing. The rosebed in the forecourt of the pub was edged with tilted bricks; she prized one out and used it to hammer at the pane of frosted glass which was the top half of the door; the glass clashed and tinkled as it fell to the floor inside. The first blow was the dangerous one, because the glass might go anywhere; after that, if you were sensible, it was quite easy to knock away the jagged lengths of pane around the central hole, until you were tapping away the last sharp splinters along the wooden rim at the bottom.

That done, Nicky took her spare skirt out of her satchel and laid it along the wood; she put her hands on the skirt, bounced twice on her toes to get the feel of the ground, and flicked herself neatly through the gap. Gym had been her best subject, once.

The saloon bar was the usual mess, with all the glasses smashed and empty bottles of beer and wine and whisky littering the floor. The room reeked of stale drink. But, as usual, the men who had roared and rioted in here a month ago had not been interested in the soft drinks, except as things to throw and fight with; there were several crates of ginger ale and lemon soda and tonic water under the bar counter. She heaved one out and started to drag it to the door. The light changed; there was a crash and a thump behind her; Gopal was sprawling across the floor, gasping and giggling, his feet still scuffling among the smashed splinters.

"Are you all right?" said Nicky. "Don't cut yourself."

"I'm less good at jumping than you are," he said, turning round to look at the door while he brushed his front with his hands. "If we turn your crate on its end we'll be able to unbolt the door. Then we can drag your loot out."

But outside the door stood Uncle Chacha Rahmta, looking serious. Kewal was hurrying up, while Neena watched anxiously from halfway down the slope.

"You are a bad little boy, Gopal," said Uncle Chacha. "You must not wander away like this. Your mother is very worried."

Probably he spoke in English so that Nicky could share in the reproof.

"It's quite safe," she said. "We're only getting some lemon soda for the children."

(She didn't tell him about the pub she'd broken into north of Shepherd's Bush where a dead man had sat, sprawled across a shiny red table, with a knife in his side.)

"It is notorious that Indian parents overprotect their children," said Kewal. "But that is what they do, Miss Nicky Gore, and you must respect their anxieties."

"All right," said Nicky. "Will you help us with this crate? There's plenty for everybody."

"But we cannot take this," said Uncle Chacha slowly. "It is not our property."

"It isn't anybody's," said Nicky. "They've all gone."

"We could put some money in the till," suggested Kewal.

"It's smashed," said Gopal. "I noticed."

Uncle Chacha walked into the pub, very careful and light on his feet, like a wild animal sniffing into a trap. He counted five green pieces of paper into a broken drawer. Kewal waved to the crowd on the hill and they gathered themselves into line of march and trooped down to the pub. Kewal explained what had happened, and half a dozen angry voices answered him, all together. Several faces looked at Nicky. The women joined in the row. Suddenly something was settled and four of the men went into the pub to fetch more crates, and cans of peanuts and cheese biscuits. The whole party settled to an impromptu picnic. The children recovered strength and began a squealing game of chain tag. The towers of empty flats brooded silent in the dusty afternoon air. The men settled into one group, and the women into another. Every half minute a mother would look up from her gossip and call to a child in words that Nicky couldn't understand, but in the tone that all mothers everywhere use when they are warning their children to be careful. Nicky, all of a sudden, felt just as lonely and left out as she had that morning on the Green, before the Sikhs had come.

"Do you not wish to join the game," said Kewal, who had appeared silently beside her. "Are you too old for that sort of thing, perhaps? Look, Gopal is playing."

"I'm too tired and hot," said Nicky, sighing to keep the crossness out of her voice. "What's the name of the language you talk among yourselves?"

"It's Punjabi—that's the normal language Sikhs use in India. Most of us speak English here, in fact I've friends who only know a few words of Punjabi, but in our family my grandmother has always insisted that even the kids have got to speak Punjabi at home. When my grandmother insists on something, it happens. Some of us used to resent it and stick to English when she wasn't around, but now, since the madness happened, we all seem to have become more Sikh. Sometimes I find myself actually thinking in Punjabi. I never used to."

"Why are you all still here? Why did you leave so late? Everybody else went away a long time ago."

"Oh," said Kewal, "at first we couldn't decide what
was happening. Some of us used to work for London
Transport, but when the early shift went to get the
buses out they were attacked by mobs of Englishmen.
Even the little children threw stones as soon as an engine started. And they weren't like you—they didn't
stop when the engines were turned off. Perhaps it was
because there were so many of them; it's difficult, you
know, for a whole crowd to stop rioting once they've
started. But none of my relations was killed, though my
cousin Surbans Singh was badly beaten. So they came
home, and the rest of us couldn't go to work because
none of the buses and trains were running. I started to
bicycle to the university—I'm a student—but I was
chased by shouting people so I came home too. We shut
ourselves in our houses—we have three houses all together in the same road—and held a council. We decided that all the English people had been infected by a
madness against machines, which for some reason did
not affect us Sikhs. Oh, now I'll tell you something
interesting and significant. The Jamaicans had also
gone to get the buses out, but my cousin Surbans said
that they were extremely clumsy and giggled all the
time when they made a mistake. He thought they'd all
been drinking—at four o'clock in the morning, which is
not impossible with Jamaicans. So perhaps they too
were a little affected by the madness, but not in the
same manner as the English. Anyway our council de-

cided that we'd wait until the madness passed. But it didn't pass. One of my uncles owns a store, so there was enough to eat, but water became difficult and sanitary arrangements too. And it was difficult to cook without . . . What's the matter, Miss Gore?"

Nicky had only been able to understand about half of what Kewal said. His explanation seemed full of nasty, fuzzy words and ideas, such as "bicycle." She felt a qualm of the old sick rage bubbling up inside her—the rage she'd felt in Castelnau, or on that first morning when Daddy had gone around the house with his hammer smashing all the nasty gadgets of their lost life. But it was only a qualm this time, not strong enough for killing or smashing. She put her head between her hands and waited for the qualm to seep away. Kewal watched her in silence.

"Please don't talk about things like that," she said at last. "You mustn't."

"Why?"

"I don't know why, but you mustn't."

He smiled.

"You're a good canary," he said. "You will be really useful to us. I must go and tell my uncles what you say."

"No, wait," said Nicky. "I think I can explain a bit more. Gopal was talking to me before, and he said things which worried me in a different kind of way. The things you were talking about made me feel very angry, very mad really. I don't mind your calling it madness, because it's just like that. But Gopal was talking about India, and the war and things which I'm sure I knew about once. But now it's . . . it's as if they'd become so . . . so *boring,* I suppose, that my brain goes to sleep before I can think about them. I couldn't remember the word for your hats until he told me it was 'turbans.' Do you understand?"

"Aha!" said Kewal, his terrible squint sparkling with pleasure at his own cleverness, "I begin to see. Shall I explain my theorem to you?"

"No, please," said Nicky, who had only just managed to struggle through the discomfort of trying to think about the shut places of her own mind. "Go and tell your uncles."

That caused further delay while the two groups of grown-ups joined to discuss Nicky; at one point a quarrel broke out and excitable fists were flung skyward, but it was all over as suddenly as a child's tantrums. Then at last they were on the march again, hauling prams and carts up the steep slope to the common, then turning right to trundle down toward Kingston. The children who had darted so eagerly through their game became tired almost at once, oppressed by the dreariness of the slow walk. By the time they came to Robin Hood Roundabout, where the road divides, one of the smallest ones was sniveling and several mothers had found space for an extra burden on their prams. Nicky helped fat Kaka up onto the old lady's cart.

"I shall not be able to push a great weight like yours except downhill," said the big man severely. Kaka grinned between fat cheeks and reached for his grandmother's hand. Or perhaps she was his great-grandmother, Nicky thought. All the grown-ups seemed to show a special kindness toward the small children, despite their strange, fierce looks.

At the roundabout a further conference was held. Nicky lounged amid the incomprehensible babble and looked north, through Robin Hood Gate, to where the green reaches of Richmond Park lay quiet in the westering sun.

"Miss Gore," a voice called. It was the big uncle.

"Yes."

"We are discussing whether we should go through Kingston or along the bypass. It is shorter to go through, although there is a big hill. Would it, shall I say, *affect* you if we went one way or the other?"

"I don't know," said Nicky. "Couldn't we go in there?"

She pointed to the inviting greenness of the park. Some of the mothers made approving noises. The discussion in Punjabi clattered out again. Really, Nicky couldn't understand how any of them could be *listening* with so many of them talking all together. This time the women seemed to have more to say than the men, but at last the noise quietened and in the lull Gopal's grandmother said something decisive. The march wheeled into the park.

"We've decided that the children have gone far enough," said Neena, "so we shall camp here for the night. The women wanted to sleep in a house, but the men said there was more danger of sickness. My mother said that we shall have to camp often, and this would be a warm fine night, with no enemies about, for practice."

"Oh, this is much nicer than houses," said Nicky.

The grass stood tall, shivering in faint slow waves under a breeze so slight that it seemed to be the sunlight itself that moved the stems. The copses looked cool and dark. A cackle of interest burst from several lips together; following the pointing arms Nicky saw a troop of deer move out of shade into sunlight. The big uncle studied his map and then led the march right to where a swift brook flowed in a banked channel.

Here, while a dozen mothers scolded children in Punjabi about the dangers of falling in, they began to set up camp, slowly, arguing about every detail, four people fussing over some easy matter while a fifth struggled alone with an unmanageable load. The fifth might shout angrily for help, but his voice went unnoticed amid the clamor.

Then, quite suddenly, everything was sorted out to everyone's satisfaction and the women started to fill pots from the stream while the men and the older boys straggled off toward the nearest copse.

"You come too, Nicky," called Gopal.

Halfway to the trees they came to a neat stack of fencing posts which the men picked up and carried back for firewood while the boys and Nicky went on.

As they reached the edge of the wood they heard a scuffling and snorting, and about twenty deer flounced away uphill, then turned to watch them from beyond throwing range.

"If only I had a gun!" said one of the older boys with a laugh. "Pow! Wump! Kerzoingg!"

"No!" cried Nicky.

"A bow and arrow, perhaps," said Gopal in a teasing voice.

"Yes, that would be all right," said Nicky, seriously.

It took them some time to gather dry twigs and branches and pile them together for dragging down to the camp. By then the men had fetched the whole pile of fencing posts and were sawing them into short logs. Soon four neat fires were sending invisible flames into the strong, slant sun. Pots boiled. Some of the men were cutting bracken up the hill, others were rigging a mysterious screen. A child fell into the stream, but luckily Kewal was sitting on the bank, brooding at the passing water, and he snatched it out. The child was scolded for falling in and Kewal for not doing his share of the work. Nicky half dozed, and wondered whether it was all a dream.

"Come and wash, Nicky," said Neena, "if you want to."

There was nothing she wanted more. The women were queueing to wash behind the screen, using barely more than a mugful of hot water each in a collapsible canvas baby bath. Nicky, ashamed at her month's grime, used more than her share of water, but nobody complained. Cousin Punam inspected her scratches and dabbed some nasty-smelling stuff along the sore place where her collar had been rubbing. Neena borrowed clean clothes for her from another mother. Then she joined the chattering laundry party.

A frowning woman, darker than the others and with flecks of gray in her hair, hung out her own clothes beside Nicky and looked at her several times without speaking.

"We Sikhs are a very clean people," she said at last, in an accusing voice. "We are cleaner than Europeans."

"I like being clean too," said Nicky.

"Good," said the woman without smiling.

Then Nicky was called over to where the men, who had also been washing and laundering, were holding a council. Gopal had told them about the gun and the bow, and now they settled down to ask her random questions about what they could or could not do with safety. It was difficult because some of the questions made her sick and unhappy again; besides, the way they all asked different questions at the same time, or started discussions in Punjabi among themselves, or became involved in flaring arguments about things that didn't seem to matter at all—all this muddled her attempts at sensible answers. If she hadn't been so tired she would have laughed at them several times, but soon she realized that it wouldn't have been a good idea. They were too proud and prickly to take kindly to being laughed at by an outsider. She thought they wouldn't actually hurt her, not now; but looking at the rich beards and the strong teeth and the dark eyes, fiery and secret, she was sure that they could be very cruel to their enemies.

And Nicky wasn't an enemy—but she was determined not to be a friend either. As the big uncle had said, she was to help them and they were to help her, but one day that would end, and it must end without hurting her. She realized that her raid on the pub had been partly a way of saying that she didn't belong, that the Sikhs had no other claims on her than the single contract of alliance. She was their canary, but she was neither friend nor enemy.

While one of the longest arguments straggled on, Nicky noticed a movement just beyond the group. Four or five deer, long accustomed to the idea that people mean picnickers, and picnickers mean scraps of food, had come nosing up. Uncle Chacha, who hadn't spoken as much as the others so far, now broke into the argument in Punjabi, shifting a couple of feet back out of the circle as he did so. The deer shied away at his movement, then drifted slowly in again.

"Do not look at them, Miss Gore," said one of the uncles. "A wild animal is made more nervous by the gaze of the hunter."

"I do wish everyone would call me Nicky," she said. "Miss Gore sounds like somebody's aunt."

Smiles glowed amid the beards.

"Okay," said several voices; but they said it quietly, and when the discussion rambled on it did so without any sudden bursts of shouting which might disturb a wild animal.

She never saw Uncle Chacha strike because she was carefully not looking straight at the deer. But in the corner of her eye there was a flash of movement, a silent explosion followed by one sharp thud. Then the deer were bounding away and all the Sikhs were on their feet, crowding around and cheering. Nicky jostled through to see what had happened and found Uncle Chacha standing, stave in hand, by what looked like a pale brown sack. He hung his head with exactly Kaka's shyness—he must be the fat boy's father. Then Nicky saw that the sack had a spindly leg, and a round eye big as a halfpenny, dull and unwinking.

"He broke its neck with his lathi," said Kewal proudly. "One blow, bim, like that. We'll have roast venison for supper."

The council was over. Nicky raced twigs on the

stream with Gopal and his friends for a bit, then joined in a game of blindman's buff. Then all the children sat in a circle around the cart to hear the old lady tell them a story. Nicky went off to play with a tiny brown baby, Neena's niece, who kicked and gurgled on a pink towel. After that she curled up and slept amid the tickling grasses.

It was almost dark when they woke her, and the dewy dusk smelled beautifully of roasted meat. They all sat on the trampled grass in a ragged circle around the fires; even the smallest babies were awake again, staring from their mothers' laps at the wavering flames. The Sikhs looked stranger still as the night deepened; the men's beards became huge shadows—shadows with no shape to cast them—and in these shadows a row of teeth would gleam for a moment when a mouth opened to talk or smile or chew; the eyes too shone weird in the weird light. They looked like a ring of pirates, murderous invaders.

The venison was charred at the edges and tough to chew, but full of delicious juices even if you did have to spit out the pithy gobbets of fiber that were left unswallowable at the end of each mouthful. The Sikhs had made a curry sauce to dip the meat into, and passed it around in pots, but it was too hot for Nicky. The grownups ate a flattish sconelike bread called chapati, which they'd brought with them, but the children preferred to finish off the cheese biscuits from the pub. The drinking water was still tepid from its boiling, but delicious after a month of lemon soda.

When they'd finished eating, the big man stood up by the old lady's cart and read in a solemn voice from a book. Sometimes the Sikhs answered him, all together.

"Prayers," whispered Gopal in Nicky's ear.

Some of the babies were asleep again before he'd finished, and now they were settled into their prams. An awning had been built over the old lady's cart, and the cut bracken piled into mounds under that and the other carts for the smaller children to sleep on. The older children and the grown-ups slept in the open, women and girls in one group, men and boys in the other. Somebody had a spare blanket to lend to Nicky. The bracken was surprisingly comfortable.

"You see?" said Neena as they were sorting themselves out. "It takes a long time to make a camp. It's a lot of work. We cannot hope to march more than ten miles a day, with the children to think about and the carts and prams to push."

"Where are you going to?" said Nicky.

"We do not know. We'll just go until we can find a place where we can live. Perhaps it is across the sea, but I hope not."

Chapter 3

GOOD LAND,
CLEAN WATER

A place where they could live.

They came to it eight days later, but did not recognize it at first. They thought it was just a sensible place to stop for a few days so that Rani, Neena's sister-in-law, could have her baby. On the left of the lane stood a raw, ugly square brick farmhouse with metal-frame windows; then, a little further up the hill, was a brick shed; then a tiny brand-new bungalow; and then, for them to camp in, an old brick farmyard built like a fort with a single gateway, an old barn down one side, and on the others single-story cattle sheds and grain stores. A hundred yards on, right on the ridge of the hill, loomed two vast new concrete barns and a cluster of grain towers. On the other side of the lane there was only a single house, opposite the farmyard. Once it had been two old cottages for farm laborers, but someone had run them together and smartened them up for an artist to live in.

He'd gone, and so had all the other people. Every house was empty. No cattle lowed for milking, no cat miaowed on any doorstep. Hundreds of birds clattered in the hedges around the artist's cottage, but the farmer had hauled out every other hedge on his land to make it easier to cultivate the flowing steppes of hay and wheat and barley that now stood rippling in the upland wind across six hundred acres.

A mile and a half down the hill you could see the tower of Felpham Church, warm brick, rising amid lindens, seeming to move nearer when the afternoon sun shone full on it, and then to drift away when a cloud shadow hit the sun. You could see only a few roofs of Felpham, although it was quite a big village. Beyond that was distance.

And the distance really was distance, although the farm stood barely a hundred and fifty feet above the plain which stretched to the northeast. For twenty miles there was nothing else as high. There were no real landmarks, except the now useless electric pylons. A double row of these swooped across the slope between the farm and the village, but Nicky tried not to see them. Instead she gazed out beyond them to the mottled leagues, blue and gray and green, that reached toward London. Though they had been settled here for weeks she felt that she still could count every footstep of the road they had come.

It was the people she remembered most. First the old tramp who had come, snuffling like a hedgehog, up to their camp on Esher Common and asked for food. The Sikhs had simply made room for him, dirty as he was, and fed him all he wanted. He must have been half crazy, for he seemed to notice no difference between them and other people, nor between these times and other times, but just mumbled and chewed, and at last lurched away into the dark without a word of thanks.

But the first real people they'd met—ordinary English people, wearing English clothes—had been at Ripley. And they'd been enemies. A dozen men and women had run out of a pub at the sound of the iron wheels on the road. For a while they'd simply stared as the march of Sikhs moved slowly past, but then one of the women had said something mocking to the men, then a man had shouted and all the men were throwing stones and bottles at the Sikhs while the women cursed and jeered. Kaka had been hit by a stone, but had managed not to cry. Nicky had rushed from the line, shouting to the men to stop it; their attitude changed, and for a moment she'd thought they'd heard her and understood, until the rear guard of the Sikhs rushed past her, staves whirling. The Englishmen had broken and run, while their women cowered against the wall. As the procession moved out of Ripley there were catcalls from behind walls, and clods of earth lobbed into the line, but no one had followed them. And the people working the fields paid no attention as they marched by, grim and silent.

They'd camped that night in a field north of Guildford, on the banks of the river Wey, and had held another council. The discussion sounded earnest and subdued, and after it a party of men had gone night-raiding into Guildford, though there'd still seemed to be plenty of food left in the cardboard boxes on the carts. (Seeing a can opened made Nicky uneasy, but the meat inside tasted all right.)

They'd decided to head for the coast, but to avoid towns and villages even if it meant going the long way around. However, the houses in the Home Counties are so close sown that they were bound to pass some of them, and at the very next hamlet two or three faces had leaned out of windows and called cheerily for news, just as though columns of bearded foreigners passed that way so often that there was nothing strange about it. So for a while they'd felt more optimistic, but as they steadily trudged the days away they'd learned that every village was different, and that the frowning ones were commoner than the smiling ones. And people seemed to have little idea of what was happening more than a mile or two from their own doors.

No more stones were thrown at them, but they had thrown some themselves. This was in their second battle, on the outskirts of Aldershot, a much nastier business than the skirmish at Ripley. The enemy had been a wandering gang of robbers, though at first they'd looked like another procession, trundling down the sunk road toward the Sikhs; but almost at once a dozen young men armed with pick helves had charged shouting and yelling, forcing the Sikhs' advance guard back against the group of women and children. Uncle Chacha had brought the rear guard up in a counterattack. While the grunts and bellows rose Nicky stared wildly around for something she could do. Gopal grabbed her elbow and pointed to the flinty chalk at the top of the embankment, and the next moment they were scrambling desperately up. There'd been seven of the children up there, screaming and hurling flints, by the time the robbers broke and ran back to where four or five dirty women had been watching the fun from among their own prams and barrows. The angry Sikhs had driven the lot of them on down the road, hitting as hard as they could. Nicky had stopped to look at the robbers' baggage, which had turned out to be a hoard of cheap looted jewelry, a lot of boxes of sweets and some moldy loaves. The Sikhs left it all where it was.

Mr. Gurchuran Singh had hurt his leg in the battle, so they'd decided to rest for a couple of days where they next found water. They had posted extra sentries that night, and after supper the big uncle, whose name was Mr. Jagindar Singh, had spoken very earnestly to Nicky.

"We think you should leave us," he said, "as soon as we next meet friendly people. You will be safer with them than with us. We propose to try to reach the sea and go away to France. We listened to the Paris radio in London, and they are free from this madness there."

"But what will you do for a canary?" Nicky had said.

"Oh, we shall be careful. You have taught us much."

"I'd rather come with you for a bit longer, Mr. Singh."

"We do not consider it wise."

"What does your mother say?"

"Ha, you have bewitched her, Nicky. She says that it is no business of ours, and that you are to make up your own mind."

Nicky had looked toward the cushioned cart and seen the bird-bright eyes watching her through the gloom.

"Please, then," she'd said. "I'd much rather stay. I don't want to have to learn to know a *new* lot of people. Have you still got the . . . the thing you listened to France with?"

"Kaka knocked it off the table and none of us knew how to mend it."

"Good."

She'd meant what she'd said about the new people. They would be English, like her, and the kindlier they were the worse it would be, day after day probing to pierce through the clumsy armor she'd built around her heart. They would try to be mothers, and fathers, and perhaps even the sisters and brothers she had never had. And only she would know, all the time, in waking nightmares as well as the deeps of dream, how such a home can be smashed in a single morning. She couldn't live through that again.

Besides, against all her reason, she had made a new friend. Kaka's elder sister Ajeet was a very quiet girl whom Nicky had at first thought was seven or eight; in fact the two of them had been born only a week apart. They had fallen into that instant, easy friendship which feels as though it had begun before any of your memories and will last until you are so old that the humped veins on the back of your hands show dark blue-purple through your wax-white skin. Ajeet's mother—Uncle Chacha's wife—was the fat frowning woman, and she seemed anxious to know about every breath her children drew, but they all seemed happy enough when you got to know them. At least she didn't try to be a mother to Nicky.

They had to move before Mr. Gurchuran Singh's leg was properly healed, because a passing horseman had shouted to them that there was plague in Aldershot. That had meant a long journey around the northern edge of that ugly, shambling town, so in the end they had come to Felpham from the north, taking eight days to get there from London. Felpham was a frowning village, but not a stone-throwing one, so they had trudged silently through and begun the long push up Strake Lane, never guessing that they were nearly home. In fact Nicky almost refused to pass the double line of pylons, because they seemed so much worse than the single ones which she'd crossed with a slight shudder before, but Gopal cajoled her under.

It had rained twice that day, and there were looming clouds about, so they were glad of the farmyard roofs and the dry hay beneath them. Four of the men pushed a cart laden with pots to Strake, two miles further along the road. There was a pond marked on the map at Strake.

It was Nicky who found the old well, which had enabled the farm to be built there in the first place. The close eye which the Sikh parents kept on their children irked her, though she didn't like to say so; but she tended to drift off and explore as soon as she had done what she could to help set up camp; it was her way of saying that she wasn't going to let herself be watched and pampered like that. Once or twice Gopal had slipped away and come with her, only to be scolded when they got back, but this time she was alone.

The artist's cottage was locked. Nose against windows, Nicky could see a low-ceilinged kitchen and another big room which had been made by knocking down several walls. Light streamed into it through a big skylight in the far roof. She didn't feel like visiting the huge barns because they'd be full of engines, and everywhere else was nothing but rippling wheat; so she sat on a low circular flint wall, topped with a line of brick, and thought about nothing much. The shouting and chatter of the encampment washed over her unheeded. The center of the flint wall was covered with a four-foot round of wood; she thought vaguely that it must be some sort of garden table, uncomfortable because you couldn't get your knees under it. She slapped the timber with her palm.

A slow boom answered, as though the whole hill were speaking, the million-year-old chalk answering her knock in tones almost too deep to hear. Each slap or rap produced the same bass reply. She got her fingers under the edge of the wood and it came up like a lid.

The hole in the center of the circle was black. It was a tunnel of night defying the gay sun. The palms of her hands went chilly as she clutched the brick rim and peered in. At first she could see nothing, but then there was a faint light, a circle of sky with a head and shoulders in the middle. The rough chalk walls dwindled down, becoming invisible in darkness before they reached the water. She dropped a stone but it fell crooked, clacking several times from wall to wall before the splash. She went to fetch Kewal.

He dropped three or four stones, with his other hand feeling his pulse. Even when the stones fell straight it seemed ages before the splash answered.

"About fifty feet to the water," he said. "If we can get it up, and if the water is good, it means we can stay here for a while. The women say that Rani's baby will be born in two or three days."

They found a rope and bucket in the sheds, but it took a lot of trial and error and a lot of many-voiced arguments before the men rigged up a method of getting a bucket down all that distance and making it lie sideways when it reached the water, so that it filled, and then tilted upright when it was full. Hauling a full bucket up from fifty feet was tiring, too, but it was better than walking to Strake. And the water when it came was so sweet and clean that Cousin Punam decided it was safe to drink without boiling.

It was Gopal who found the corn. While Rani was in labor, three days later, the older children were shushed away. Nicky didn't follow them up to the big barns because she felt uncomfortable there. She was looking, with little luck, for late wild strawberries in the matted grass on the banks of the lane when Gopal came hurrying past, his hands cupped close together as if he was trying to carry water. Nicky thought he'd caught a bird and ran to look.

"Nicky, you're thick," he said. "This is *food*. I climbed an iron ladder up one of those round towers and opened a lid at the top and it's full of corn. There's enough to feed us for a year. Look, it's dry and good."

He ran on to show his treasure to the menfolk, while

Nicky returned to combing through the weeds for strawberries. She found no more of the little red globules of sweetness, but caught a grasshopper instead, let it tickle her prisoning palms for a moment, then held it free and watched it tense itself for its leap, and vanish.

The baby was born in a cow stall. It was a boy. That night the Sikhs held full council. It was just as noisy and muddled with cross talk as any of the ones they'd heard on the road, but Nicky got the feeling that even in the middle of rowdy arguments they were being more serious, paying more attention to what the others said. From time to time they would ask her a question.

"We can't use any of the tractors, can we, Nicky?"

She shook her head.

"But we can reap and plow and dig and plant by hand?"

"Oh yes."

"And there's nothing wrong with this wheat?"

"Wrong?" She looked through the gateway to where the beautiful tall blades waved, gray as fungus under the big moon, but already tinged with yellow by daylight as the year edged toward harvest.

"Oh yes," said Mr. Surbans Singh, "this is a modern crossbred variety of wheat, and another of barley. The madness does not apply to them, you think?"

"Oh no!"

Another long fusillade of Punjabi followed. Then . . .

"Nicky, would the madness make the villagers come and destroy us if we were to set up a blacksmith's shop?"

"What would you do?"

"Make and mend spades and sickles and plows and other tools."

"I mean, how would you do it? What would you use?"

"We'd have to make charcoal first, which is done by burning wood very slowly under a mound of earth. Then we'd have to contrive a furnace, with bellows to keep the charcoal burning fiercely. And when the iron was red-hot we'd hammer it, and bend it with vises and pincers, and then temper it in water or oil."

"Water," said Nicky. "Where would you get the iron from?"

"There is plenty lying around the farm."

"I *think* that would be all right. You could try, and I could always tell you if I thought it wasn't. Why do you want to know?"

"First, because if we are to stay here we shall need hand tools. This farm is highly mechanized, which is no doubt why the farmer left; he felt he couldn't work it without his tractors. But secondly, we shall need more to eat than wheat. We shall have to barter for meat and vegetables until we can produce our own. Some of us have seen smithwork done in India, in very primitive conditions; Mr. Jagindar Singh was a skilled metalworker in London, and two more of us have done similar work in factories and garages; so we think we can set up an efficient smithy. But perhaps the villagers will not have our advantages, so we shall be able to barter metalwork with them in exchange for the things we need."

"That's a good idea," said Nicky, astonished again by the amount of sense that seemed to come out of all the clamor and repetition. "But do you think the villagers will actually trade with you? They didn't look very friendly when we came through, and they haven't come up here at all."

"If we make something they need, they will trade with us," said Uncle Jagindar somberly. "It does not matter how much they dislike us. We have found this in other times."

The whole council muttered agreement. Kewal gave a sharp, snorting laugh which Nicky hadn't heard before.

"We must be careful," he said. "If we become too rich they will want to take our wealth away from us."

"I expect there are quite a lot of robbers in England now," said Nicky. "Like those ones we fought on the other side of Aldershot—men who've got no way of getting food except by robbing the ones who have."

This set off another round of argument and discussion in Punjabi. The men seemed to become very excited; voices rose, eyes flashed, an insignificant uncle even beat his chest. Nicky edged back out of the circle to ask Gopal what they were talking about. He was allowed at the council, but he was thought too young to speak (Nicky wouldn't have been listened to either if she hadn't been the Sikh's canary).

Gopal laughed scornfully, but he looked as excited as the rest.

"They are going to make weapons," he said. "Swords and spears and steel-tipped arrows. A Sikh should carry a real sword when times are dangerous. But I'll tell you a joke—we Sikhs won most of our battles with guns; we used to run forward, fire a volley and then run back until we had time to reload. It doesn't sound very brave, but all India feared us then. What's the matter, Nicky? Oh, I'm sorry, I forgot. But they won't make guns now; instead they'll turn this farmyard into a fort which we can defend against the robbers."

After that the council became less serious, dwindling into boastings and warlike imaginings. Gopal translated the louder bits.

"My Uncle Gurchuran says we must capture horses and turn ourselves into cavalry, and then we can protect the whole countryside for a fee. A protection racket. We often lived like that in the old days. . . . Mr. Parnad Singh says his father was Risaldar at an archery club in Simla, and he will teach us all to shoot. A risaldar is a sort of sergeant. . . . My Uncle Chacha is teasing him and Mr. Parnad Singh is angry. . . . My Uncle Jagindar is trying to smooth him down; he says it will be useful to have a good shot with a bow for hunting, and that Uncle Chacha must be careful what he says, because he is so fat that he'll make an easy target. That's unfair because Uncle Chacha is the quickest of them all, and the best fighter. You saw how he fought against those robbers. Now he's pretending to be angry with Uncle Jagindar, but *that* doesn't matter because it's inside the family. . . . My grandmother is speaking. She says we must all be careful how we talk to one another, because we are in a dangerous world and we can't afford to have feuds with one another. My goodness, she says, we Sikhs are a quick-tempered people. She's beginning to tell a story. She tells pretty good stories, for children and adults too."

The council had fallen silent at the creak of the old woman's voice. There had been a brief guffaw of laughter at her second sentence, but that was all. One of the men turned to glare at Gopal because his translation was spoiling the silence. He too stopped talking.

The story was not long, but the old woman told it with careful and elaborate gestures of the hands, as though she were the storyteller at some great court and had been sent for after supper to entertain the princes. Nicky could hear, even in the unknown language, that it was the story of a fierce quarrel between two proud men. She looked along the outer circle of children and saw Ajeet sitting entranced, mouth slightly parted and head craning forward as she listened and stared at the elaborate ceremony of the fluttering hands. Ajeet's lips were moving with the words, and her hands made faint unconscious efforts to flutter themselves.

All the Sikhs laughed when the story ended, then broke into smaller chattering groups. Nicky crossed to where Ajeet still sat staring at the orange firelight.

"What was the story about, Ajeet?" she said.

"Oh, I don't know," said Ajeet in her usual near whisper, shy and confused.

"Please tell me. I like to know anything your grandmother says. She is so . . . so special."

"Oh, it was a tale of two Sikh brothers, farmers, whom my grandmother knew in India, and how they quarreled over a dead pigeon, and in the end lost their farm and their wives and everything. Listen. It was like this."

Her voice changed and strengthened. She drew her head back and sat very upright, freeing her hands for gestures. The history of that forgotten feud rolled out in vivid, exact words, each phrase underlined with just the same gesture of finger or wrist that her grandmother had used. Once or twice she hesitated over a word, and Nicky realized that she was turning familiar Punjabi into English which didn't quite fit. When she finished Nicky found herself laughing at the ridiculous disaster, just as the men had laughed, and heard more voices laughing behind her. Kewal and three of the other men had been standing around in silence to hear the same story all over again.

"Very excellent," said Kewal, only half mocking.

One of the men called in Punjabi over his shoulder, and was answered by a pleased cackle from the open stall where the old woman lay on her cushions; she had been watching the show too. Ajeet accepted the compliments gravely, without any of her usual shyness, then took Nicky off to say good night to the old lady.

This had become a sort of ritual for Nicky, a good-luck thing, wherever they were. They couldn't say much to each other, even with Ajeet to translate, because their lives had been so different, but somehow it ended the day on a comfortable note.

As they crossed the yard back to the shed where the women slept, Nicky looked around the firelit walls and the black-shadowed crannies. So this was home, now.

Provided nobody came to drive them out.

They settled in slowly. The bungalow had been left unlocked, and the first thing the Sikhs did was to redecorate the bedroom with rich hangings. They took their shoes off when they went into the room. Uncle Jagindar carried the old lady in when it was finished, and she clucked her satisfaction, though she wanted several details changed. Nicky watched fascinated from the doorway.

"It is a place to keep our holy book," explained Kewal. "My family are very orthodox Sikhs. Before these troubles some of us younger ones didn't treat our religion as earnestly as the elders, but now it seems more important. It will help to keep us together."

"We'll have to use the other houses to sleep in when the winter comes," said Nicky. "It'll be too cold to sleep out in the sheds."

"You are very practical-minded. That was how the English ruled India. They would go and admire the Taj Mahal, but all the time they were thinking about drains. Anyway, my uncles don't feel it proper to break into other people's houses, even if the people have gone away."

"They'll have to in the end," said Nicky. "I don't mind doing the burgling, and then once the doors are open you could all come and use the houses like you are doing this one."

Kewal laughed and pulled his glossy beard.

"That would be an acceptable compromise," he said. "But I think we won't tell my uncles until you've done it. I will attend and supervise, because in my opinion your techniques of burglary are a little crude."

But you have to be crude with metal-framed windows. They fit too tight for you to be able to slide a knife or wire through to loose the catch. Nicky broke two panes, opened two windows, climbed into two musty and silent houses, and tiptoed through the dank air to unbolt two doors. The artist's cottage was full of lovely bric-a-brac—a deer head, and straw ornaments that were made for the finials of hayricks, and Trinidadian steel drums. Kewal delightedly began to tonk out a pop tune, but Nicky (frightened now of what she'd done) dragged him away.

And the uncles *were* cross when she told them. (She left Kewal out of her story.) But when the women found that there was an open hearth in the cottage and a big closed stove in the farmhouse, in both of which you could burn logs, they told the uncles to stop being so high-minded. Here was somewhere to bathe and attend to small babies in the warm. And though the electric cookers were useless, a little bricklaying would turn the artist's drawing-room fireplace into a primitive but practical oven and stove for a communal kitchen.

Even so, Uncle Jagindar spoke very seriously to Nicky.

"It is difficult for us," he said. "If you were my child, or one of my nieces, I would punish you for this. Perhaps you are right and we will have to use these houses in winter, but you are wrong to take decisions on your own account against the wishes of us older people. If you continue to do this, then perhaps our own children will start to copy you, and then we will have to send you away. We will be sad, but we will do it."

"I'm sorry," said Nicky. "My own family weren't so . . . so . . ."

"If your own family were more like us," said Uncle Jagindar, "you would not have become separated from them as you did, even though a mad priest caused a panic."

Nicky was surprised. Ajeet was the only person she'd told about that wild Dervish who'd pranced red-eyed beside the retreating Londoners yelling about fire and brimstone; and the thunderstorm; and the hideous mass panic; and the long, sick misery of loss. Ajeet must have told her frowning mother, who must have passed the story on. But Uncle Jagindar was being unfair— anybody could have got lost in that screaming mob.

"All right," she said. "I'll try not to be a bad influence." That was her own joke—Miss Calthrop at school used to talk about girls who were bad influences, but had spoiled her case by always picking on the girls who were most fun to be with. Uncle Jagindar nodded, and Nicky went up across the fields to the wood to see how the charcoal burners were getting on.

They had made an eight-foot pyramid of logs, covered them with wet bracken, and then sealed the pile with ashes and burned earth. Then the pile was lit by the tedious process of dropping embers down the central funnel and carefully blocking them in with straight sticks. A pockmarked man was in charge, because he had done the job in India. Nicky hardly knew him, as he was one of the Sikhs who was not related to the main families and spoke little English; but now he leaned on his spade by the water hole he had dug and gave orders to the two men who were building a second pyramid of logs.

Gopal came into the clearing with his father, shoving a handcart laden with more logs for the pile.

"Wouldn't it be better sense to burn the charcoal near the log stack?" said Nicky. "Or to cut your wood from these trees here?"

"Wrong both times," said Gopal. "Nought out of ten. You must have seasoned wood, and we were lucky to find that big stack up by the road. And you must have water to quench the charcoal with when you take the pile to bits. If Mr. Harbans Singh hadn't found that spring, we might have had to carry the wood all the way down to the well."

"How long before you get any charcoal?"

"Three days, Mr. Harbans says, but the first lot may not be very good. Have you finished your bow, Risaldar?"

They all called Mr. Parnad Singh Risaldar now. It was a joke in a way, but he seemed to like it. Perhaps it reminded him of the glories of his father's Simla club. He was an older man than the others, his beard a splendid gray waterfall. He looked up from where he was whittling at a long stave.

"In a year's time, perhaps," he said, "unless I can find some seasoned ash or yew before then. With something like this, I'd be lucky to kill a rabbit at twenty paces. But tell me, Nicky—if I used tempered steel from the farmyard—the right piece, I mean—would it be safe to use that?"

"I think so," said Nicky uncertainly.

"Let's try," said Gopal. "There's all sorts of metal littered about the barn."

Halfway down the huge field two bright-colored figures were working, a man in a crimson turban and a woman in an orange sari. When the children came nearer they saw that it was Mr. Surbans Singh and his wife Mohindar, he scything, she raking. Mr. Surbans Singh had appointed himself head farmer.

"What are you doing?" called Gopal.

Mr. Surbans Singh straightened up, but his wife (whom Nicky thought the prettiest of all the Sikhs) went on tedding the grass he'd cut into a loose line.

"I found this scythe in a shed," he said. "It is very bad, and the hay is grown too coarse to be good feed, but poor hay will be better than none if we are to keep sheep through the winter."

"Sheep?" said Nicky, surprised.

"I hope so," said Mr. Surbans Singh. "I would not like to eat nothing but chapati all the year round. Eh, my dear?"

Mrs. Mohindar stopped raking and smiled at him.

"I have married a greedy man," she said.

Mr. Surbans Singh looked at the tiny patch he had cut, and then at the vast sweep of the hayfield.

"We have a long way to go," he said ruefully, and bent to his scything.

From the gray-white hulk of the barns came an erratic clinking of metal. Nicky noticed Gopal looking at her out of the corner of his eye as they walked down the slope.

"What are they up to?" she said nervously.

"Come and see."

She wouldn't actually go in under the big roof, but the barn was open at both ends and she could see the whole scene. All down one side a rank of bright-colored engines, gawky with insectlike joints and limbs, stood silent. Other machines and parts of machines littered the floor of the barn, leaving only just enough passage-way for the tractors to haul the attachments they needed in and out.

"This farmer liked gadgets," said Gopal. "Three combines, two hay balers, six different tractors, all the latest devices."

"What are the men doing?" said Nicky, quivering.

Uncle Jagindar was walking about among the engines with a hammer. From time to time he would tap at one, which produced the clinking, and call a man over to him, point and explain.

"Iron and steel are funny stuff," said Gopal. "There are lots of different kinds. Some you can work with, and some you can't—it is too hard, or its softening point is too high, or it comes from the forge too brittle. My

Uncle Jagindar wants ordinary mild steel, and he's looking for bits he can use; the others are trying to take them off the tractors and attachments."

"And the things won't go when they're taken to bits?" said Nicky.

"That would suit you?"

"Yes, but it's not as good as smashing them."

She was quite serious, but Gopal laughed and Uncle Jagindar heard the noise and came out into the sunlight. He was interested in the idea about the bow, but said he didn't think they'd find steel whippy enough, and he didn't think he could temper a rod to that state either. Besides, it would be very dangerous to the bowman if it snapped under tension. Then he shouted to one of the men, who brought out an old sickle without a handle which they'd unearthed. Uncle Jagindar sharpened it with a stone and bound sacking tightly around the tang until it was comfortable to hold. Gopal, much to his disgust, was sent up to help Mr. Surbans Singh in the hayfield, and Nicky went with him to turn the hay.

It was surprising how much got cut, provided you didn't stop every few minutes to look and see how you were getting on.

Chapter 4

STEEL ON THE ANVIL

Eight days later Nicky went down to the village. She bent her head and ran with a shudder of disgust under the double set of power lines that swooped from pylon to pylon across the lane.

"You are afraid that they will fall on you?" asked Uncle Chacha, rolling cat-footed beside her.

"No, it isn't that. But they feel like a . . . like a curse."

"Probably that is why the village people have not come up to disturb us, then."

"I expect so."

In fact she could see a whole party of villagers in a

field up to their right, almost half a mile away. They were loading a wagon with hay; the wagon was pulled by eight ponies. She pointed.

"They've quite enough fields to work on near the village," she said, "without coming up our way."

"It is curious that they are all working together," said Uncle Chacha. "I would have expected them to be cultivating separate patches—that is more the English style. Perhaps somebody has organized them."

He walked on the verge, keeping close in under the ragged hedge. He was wearing his dull green turban, for extra camouflage. They stopped about fifty yards from the first house, and he tucked himself in behind a bulge of hawthorn.

"If you are in trouble, run this way," he said. "But I will not come to help you unless you scream or call."

"All right," said Nicky. "But I'm sure you needn't worry."

She walked on. It had taken a lot of argument at the council before the Sikhs had agreed that the best way to make contact with the village was for her to go down alone and try to find somebody to talk to. Most of the women had thought it was dangerous, and the men had also felt that it was dishonorable to let a girl take the risk. But the old grandmother had been her ally in the argument, and together they'd won.

The first few houses were larger than cottages and looked empty. In front of one of them was a small paddock littered with striped pony jumps. The next houses were smaller and looked lived in, but there was no sign of life. She rounded the corner into the wider bit of road which is called the Borough, and there, under the inn sign of the Five Bells, three men sat on a bench with pewter mugs in their hands.

They looked up as soon as they heard her footfall.

"Good morning," said Nicky.

The nearest man pushed a battered brown felt hat back over his short-cropped gray hair. His face was brown with sun, and his small gray eyes sharp and suspicious. But he spoke friendly enough.

"And good morning to you, miss," he said. "Where're you from, then?"

"I'm staying on the farm up the hill," said Nicky.

The group tensed. A lean-faced young man with a half-grown beard said, "Booker's Farm, that'd be?"

"I don't know its name," said Nicky. "We just came there and stayed because one of my friends was going to have a baby."

"How many o' you?" said the hat wearer.

"About forty."

They looked at each other.

"That's them," said a little old man in shirt sleeves. He spoke with an odd, crowing note.

The others nodded.

"I know what," said the beard grower. "They kep' her prisoner and now she's run away and come to us."

"No," said Nicky. "They helped me get out of London, and so I stayed with them."

"Bad place, London," said the man in the hat.

"You aren't one on 'em, though?" crowed the man in shirt sleeves.

"No," said Nicky. "They're called Sikhs."

"Know what we call 'em?" said the man in the hat. "We call 'em the Devil's Children."

"But they aren't like that at all," said Nicky.

"Leastways they aren't like other folk," said the man in the hat. "Not like good Christian folk. You grant me that."

"They've been very good to me," said Nicky.

"That's as may be," said the man in shirt sleeves. "We don't want nothing to do with 'em. That's what the Master tells us, and he's right again, too."

"Is there a smith in the village?" said Nicky.

"Neither there isn't," said the man in the hat. "And if there was, he wouldn't care to work for the Devil's Children, would he now?"

The men seemed to become more hostile and suspicious every word they spoke.

"Oh, *we* don't need a smith," she said. "But we thought *you* might. For making plows and mending spades and things like that. The Sikhs are very good smiths."

She hoped that was true. The first furnace hadn't blown hot enough, and had had to be rebuilt. But the big double bellows had been fashioned from wood and canvas and proved to spout a steady blast of air; and though the first mound of charcoal opened had been poor stuff, and the second not much better, they were all delighted with the product of the new one which had been built on the site of the first.

The three villagers looked at each other, and the one in shirt sleeves rose to his feet.

"Perhaps I'd best go and fetch him, then," he said.

"Right you are, Maxie," said the man in the hat. Maxie scuttled away around the corner.

"And you'd best be up the hayfield, Dunc," said the man in the hat, "afore he finds you sitting here swilling of a morning."

The beard grower stood up too, but didn't leave.

"Funny thing," he said. "I remember my granny telling me stories about the Queer Folk, and as often as not they was smiths and ironworkers. Under the hills they used to live then, she said."

"That's a fact," said the man in the hat. "I remember that too. Not as I actually thought on it for years and years, but maybe there's something in it. Maybe they went up to London after."

"They'll bring you luck, if only you don't cross 'em," said the beard grower eagerly.

"Best have nothing to do with them," said the man in the hat.

"But good iron they made," said the beard grower. "Never wore out, my granny told me."

Yes, thought Nicky, it would be easy to believe the Sikhs were some sort of hobgoblins, if living with them day by day didn't keep reminding you that they were ordinary people—bones and veins and muscles and fat. Even she could only recall in shifting glimpses that other world, before all these changes happened, where you actually *knew* about Sikhs and foreigners without (perhaps) ever having met any. But these fancies were going to make barter difficult. On the other hand it meant that the villagers were less likely to come raiding up to the farm. . . .

She was still hesitating what to say next when the little man, Maxie, came back.

Beside him strode a giant. A man seven feet tall, red-faced and blue-eyed. He had no waist at all, but a broad leather belt held shirt and trousers together at the equator of his prodigious torso. Another strap hung across his shoulder and from it dangled a naked cutlass. His cheeks were so fat that separate pads of brick-red flesh bobbled below his eye sockets. Nicky noticed that the man in the hat had stood up when he appeared. The other man, the beard grower, was already standing, and it was at him that the giant stared.

" 'Morning, Arthur," said the man in the hat.

"What you doing down here, Dunc?" said the giant.

"The rest of 'em's up at the hayfield. Them as don't work this summer won't eat this winter."

"Right you are, Arthur," said the beard grower. "My foot's been playing me up, but it's better now."

He slipped away, and the blue gaze turned itself on Nicky.

"Who's this, then?" said the giant. His voice was a slow purr, like a well-fed tabby's.

"She says as she lives with the Devil's Children," explained the man in the hat. "And she says as they've blacksmiths up there, willing to make and mend for us."

"So Maxie told me," said the giant. "You think we got nothing to do but break good tools, miss?"

"Oh no," said Nicky. "But however careful you are, things do get broken, and it isn't going to be so easy to mend them now, or to buy new ones. And I expect there are things you haven't got, like plows which you can pull by hand or behind a horse. All the plows up at the farm are made for pulling behind those . . . you know . . . tractors."

As she got the nasty word out the giant took a quick pace forward. She saw a pink thing wheeling toward her but before she had time to duck, his open palm, large as a dish, smacked into the side of her head and sent her sprawling. She hadn't even stopped her scraping slide across the dusty tarmac when her shoulders were seized and she was lifted into the air.

She opened her eyes and through the dizziness and

tears she saw that the giant was holding her at arm's length, three feet above the ground, so that his face was directly opposite hers. He began to shake her to and fro. As he shook he spoke, in just the same purring voice.

"I'll have no talk *(shake)* like that *(shake)* in my village *(shake)*. Not one word of it *(shake)*. D'you hear *(shake)*? I'll have no talk *(shake)* like that *(shake)* in my village."

"Easy, Arthur, easy!" The little man was hanging on to the giant's left elbow. His weight seemed to make no difference at all to the shaking.

"She's only a kid," crowed the little man, as though he were speaking to the deaf.

The giant stopped shaking and put Nicky down.

"I'd treat my own kids a sight rougher if I heard 'em talking that kind of filth," he purred.

"But what d'you make of what she was saying before?" said the man in the hat. "I got a spud-fork needs a good weld. And we'll be crying for hand plows come seed time."

"Fetch her your fork then," said the giant. "Let's see what sort of a job they do. And then maybe they can show us a plowshare. You, girl, they'll be wanting something out of us in exchange, won't they, or my name's not Arthur Barnard."

The vast forefinger pointed suddenly at Nicky as though she'd been trying to cheat him.

"Milk and vegetables and vegetable seed for next

year and meat," she gabbled. "Not beef. They aren't allowed to eat beef in their religion."

"Heathen," purred the giant. "I'm not having them come among *my* streets, not with fifty plows. Fetch her your fork, Tom, and let's see what kind of a job they make of it."

He turned on his heel and strolled away with four-foot paces. The man and the girl watched him until he was out of earshot.

"Sorry he hit you like that, miss, but it was your fault for talking nastiness."

"Yes. Shall I call you Mr. Tom?"

"That'll do. Tom Pritchard's me full name."

"But who is *he?*"

"Arthur Barnard. The Master we call him now. Time was Felpham was full of a different crowd of folk—men went up to London most days, children went away to school, women didn't have enough to do. So *they* ran the village. Then they left, all of a sudden, and only us kind of folk remained. Soon after that a band of ruffians come along, more than twenty of 'em, came here to break and steal and to gobble what food we had. They were that fierce and that rough that most of us were scared to stand up to 'em, but Arthur Barnard—cow-man he used to be, up at Ironside's—he drove 'em out. Took that sword he wears out of the old admiral's cottage and drove 'em out. Pretty nigh on single-handed he did it. Since then what he says goes, like as you've seen. You come with me, miss, and we'll find that fork."

He limped away to his council house up beyond the church. The fork had been broken just above where the handle joined the tines. One long strip of iron still ran up the front of the wood, but the wood itself was snapped and the strip of iron behind had rusted right through.

Uncle Chacha turned the tool over discontentedly in the shelter of the hedge and listened to Nicky's story.

"I don't know," he said. "Perhaps Jagindar can mend it, but it doesn't look easy. This is not my trade; I am a checker in a warehouse, not a blacksmith. Does your head hurt where the man hit you?"

"I'm getting used to being hit," said Nicky, fingering the bruised bone. "He wasn't quite so quick as you are, but his hand was much heavier."

Uncle Chacha nodded, put the fork over his shoulder and started on the trudge up the lane. After a while he said, "This man sounds interesting. A smaller fighter can sometimes defeat a bigger one because he is quicker, but a man who is very big and quite quick will usually win."

"If you were a checker in a warehouse," said Nicky, "how do you know so much about fighting, and why are you so good at it?"

"I am very quick," said Uncle Chacha, "because all my life I have played squash. I am quite good—I have played in the national championships, though I didn't get very far. I have also learned some judo, because I was not very popular at the warehouse when I first went there. The other men were racially intolerant, and I wished to be able to defend myself. A Sikh should know how to fight."

"But swords and things," said Nicky.

"Oh, we will have to see."

They got the forge going properly two days later. Nicky stood in the doorway of the shed, where the stolid sun beat brilliant against the brick, and watched a pair of uncles pumping rhythmically at the bellows bar in the dusky interior. The pulses of air roared with a deep, hungry note as they drove through the glowing charcoal, turning it from dull red to orange and from orange to searing yellow. Uncle Jagindar stood in the orange cone of light from the furnace door, shading his eyes as he gazed against the glare. He was stripped to the waist and the weird light cast blue shadows between the ridges of his muscles. At last he grunted and nodded, and Mr. Gurchuran Singh picked up a pair of pincers and lifted a short bar of white-hot metal from the furnace. When it was firm on the anvil Uncle Jagindar smote steadily at it with a four-pound hammer. The brightness died out of it as though the blows were killing the light; the crash of each blow rang so sharp, and the next crash followed it so quickly, that Nicky's head began to ring with the racket and she put her hands to her ears. Kewal took her by the elbow and led her away.

"Is it all right?" he said. His anxiety seemed to make his squint worse than ever.

"Oh yes," said Nicky. "Only it's so *noisy*. What are they making?"

"Just a practice piece, a small sword for one of the children. It may not be very good because Jagindar isn't sure of the quality of the steel he is using. Steel is a mixture of iron and carbon in exact quantities, and the hot charcoal adds more carbon to the iron, so you achieve steel of a different temper. In primitive conditions like this it is all a matter of judgment, so the first few things he makes will probably be flawed or brittle."

Nicky looked down the slope to where two extraordinary figures were prancing on the unmown lawn behind the farmhouse. Their padded necks and shoulders made them look heavy and gawky, but they skipped around each other like hares in March, taking vicious swipes at the padding with short, curved staves. Few of the swipes reached their target because the figures ducked and backed so agilely, or took the blow cunningly on the little round leather shields which Uncle Chacha had cut from old trunks in the farmhouse attic. Suddenly Nicky realized that the six-yard folds of fine linen from which the Sikhs contrived their turbans would be almost as useful in battle as a steel helmet. The fencing practice stopped, and Uncle Chacha and

Mr. Harbans Singh leaned on their staves and discussed what they had learned.

"Yes," said Nicky, "I suppose a brittle sword wouldn't last long with that amount of bashing. But I thought proper fencers prodded at each other with the points of their swords, instead of swiping like that."

"It's a different type of sword," said Kewal. "We Sikhs have always used the tulwar, which you call a saber. The curve of the blade helps the cutting edge to slice through whatever you strike at. You Europeans invented the dueling sword, using the point to pierce your enemy before he could reach you, but even European cavalry has always used the saber, because the horse carries a man to close quarters where the cutting edge is handier than the point."

"I hope he doesn't make Mr. Tom's fork brittle," said Nicky. "Let's go and help in the hayfield."

Kewal made a face, but walked up the path beside her. Nicky was learning all sorts of surprising differences between the Sikhs, who had at first seemed so like each other. Kewal, for instance, was quick and clever, but lazy and vain; most days he seemed to have some reason to wear his smartest clothes, and the clothes then became a reason for not doing any hard or dirty work—though he was usually on the fringe of any working party, criticizing and giving advice. If Nicky had suggested going up to the wood to help in the endless job of carting charcoal down to the forge, he'd have found a reason for doing something else. The black and brittle treasure from the opened mounds filled all the air around with a fine and filthy dust. That was work too dirty for Kewal.

Suddenly Nicky laughed aloud. *She* was going up to the hayfield as an excuse for not taking her turn at the flour milling, which she thought the dreariest job on the whole farm: you pounded and rubbed and sieved for an hour, and finished with two cupfuls. Kewal looked to see if she would share the joke, but she shook her head.

The toy sword was given to Kaka, and he swaggered about with it stuck into his straining belt, looking just like a miniature version of the giant down in the village. Uncle Jagindar was pleased with it, because it didn't snap when you bent it or banged the anvil with it, and the edge came up killing sharp. He practiced all next day at the forge and on the third day he mended Mr. Tom's fork, welding a new length of steel up the back. The risaldar shaped a new handle, and the finished job looked almost as good as a fork from a shop. Nicky was ready to take it down at once, but Gopal said, "No, listen!"

The bells were going in the church tower, tumbling sweetly through their changes. It must be Sunday. The Sikhs didn't keep Sunday or any other day as special; instead they had long prayers and readings from their holy book morning and evening. Yes, it would be a mistake to go down on a Sunday, another sign of how different the two communities were.

She found Mr. Tom at his house on Monday morning. He fingered the weld and the new handle with hands so harsh that you could hear his skin scrape across the surface.

"Clean and sturdy, I'd say," he said. "We'll show the Master. He's in court, Mondays."

They found the giant in what had been a classroom in the school. Mr. Tom led Nicky quietly in and pointed to a bench where she could sit. Twenty other villagers were there, cramped behind child-sized desks; the giant sat up on the dais, also cramped, though his desk had been made for a grown man. Maxie sat at a table below the dais, scribbling in a ledger. A dark, angry-looking woman stood in front of the desk complaining about something. When she stopped she sat down. The giant looked at the room in silence for a full minute.

Then he nodded to Maxie, who had stopped writing. Maxie leaped to his feet and crowed like a cock.

"Now hear this!" were the words he crowed. The giant purred into the silence.

"Mrs. Sallow," he said, "has brought a complaint against her neighbor Mr. Goddard, saying that his dog spoils her flower beds by burying bones in 'em. There are three points to this case. Firstly, it is the nature of a dog to bury its bones where it feels like, and you can't change that. Secondly, flower beds aren't of no account in Felpham no more—it's vegetables we'll be needing, beans and such, to see us through the coming winter. Thirdly, which falls into two parts, a man must have a good dog, and if that dog goes digging up the neighbor's flower beds the neighbor has to put up with it, though it would be different, like I said, if it was vegetables. And moreover it is the use and custom of Felpham that a woman is subservient to a man, and when it comes to a complaint, other things being equal, the man shall have the best of it. Case dismissed."

"Case dismissed," crowed Maxie, and began to scribble again in his ledger.

The dark woman, looking angrier than ever, bustled out of the classroom.

"That's the last case, eh, Maxie?" said the giant.

"Yessir."

Mr. Tom stood up.

"The girl's brought my spud fork back from the Devil's Children," he said. "Seems like a good mend to me."

"Let's have a squint at it," said the giant.

Tom took the fork up to the dais and the giant rose from his desk. First he waggled the tool to and fro in his huge hands, then he peered at the actual join, then he took the tines in one hand and the handle in the other, put his knee to the join and heaved.

"Oi!" cried Mr. Tom. "Don't you go busting of it, Arthur!"

The giant stopped heaving and gazed at Mr. Tom from under reddish eyebrows. Mr. Tom looked away, and the giant resumed heaving. Nicky could see the squares of his checked shirt change shape where they crossed his shoulders as the oxlike muscles bulged with the effort. The classroom was silent as a funeral. Suddenly there came a crack and a twang, and the fork changed shape.

The giant straightened and held it up. He had snapped the wooden handle clean in two, and one of the steel supports had broken with it, but the other had held. It was the piece Uncle Jagindar had mended which had stayed unbroken.

"Now hear this," purred the giant, panting slightly with the aftermath of that great spasm of strength.

"Now hear this!" crowed Maxie.

"We'll be needing a fair whack of honest tools," said the giant. "Some will want mending, and some we haven't got. You all know how the Devil's Children have settled in up at Booker's, and how near we came to raiding up there and driving 'em out, bad wires or no bad wires. Now it turns out that they've blacksmiths among them, as will make and mend ironwork for us, and do an honest job at it. So I say this: if a man wants a piece of iron mended, or made, he'll come to me and tell me what he wants, and I'll fix a fair price for him with this girl here as lives with the Devil's Children. If you want a job done, you must pay a fair price. But I won't fix a price which the village or the man can't spare, I promise you that. It'll be a bag of carrots, maybe, for a mended spade, and a lamb or two for a new plow. And I hereby appoint Tom Pritchard my deputy to handle this trade, seeing as I broke your fork, Tom, though I'll oversee it myself till we've got it running smoothly. But if I find one of you, or any other man or woman in Felpham, dealing with the Devil's Children direct, other than through me or Tom Pritchard and this girl here, I'll skin 'em alive, I promise you that. We have to trade with 'em, but they're heathen, outlandish heathen, and apart from trade we don't want to see nor hide nor hair of 'em. I've heard some of you talking fancy about them, saying as they're the Queer Folk and suchlike rubbish. I don't want to hear no more of that. They're mortal flesh, like you and me. But they're heathen foreigners besides, and it is the use and custom of Felpham to have nothing to do with 'em. Now, such of you as've got metal to make and mend, you're to bring it to the Borough, or drawings of what you want. Maxie, you can cry the news through the village. Court adjourned."

"Court adjourned," crowed Maxie, and whisked out of the room like a blown leaf. Tom went ruefully up to the dais to collect his ruined fork; Nicky saw that he was too afraid of the giant to complain. She sat where she was while the room cleared; all the time the giant stared at the wall above the door, as though he could see through it.

When the last of the villagers had gone he yawned, scratched the back of his head, stood up, settled his cutlass strap over his shoulder, covered it with an orange cloak which he pinned in place with a big brooch, clapped a broad hat with a plume in it onto his head and strode toward the door. Nicky saw that he was wearing boots now, and that the cloak had once been a curtain. The room boomed at every footfall. He stopped suddenly, as though he'd only just noticed her.

"What are you waiting for, girl?" he said.

"I wanted to ask you how we're going to fix a proper price for the work if you won't meet any of the Sikhs."

"The Devil's Children," he said.

"They aren't like that at all," said Nicky. "They're proud, and they wear funny clothes, and they talk a lot, but when you get to know them they're really like anybody else. Just ordinary."

"None of my folk's going to get to know the Devil's Children," said the giant without looking at her. "But I give you my honor I'll strike a fair price. Think, girl, it's in my interest till we can find a smith of our own; there's a heap of metalwork to be done before winter if we're to come through it short of starving. I don't want your people trading over to Aston, nor Fadlingfield, because they think we've cheated 'em here. Now you run along. This afternoon I'll send a barrow of stuff up as far as the bad wires; you can fetch it back, mended, this day week. We're vicious short on scythes, too, so you can get your friends to forge us half a dozen new 'uns—we'll shape the handles."

"All right," said Nicky, and turned to go.

"Come back, girl," said the giant. "I've more to say. You heard what I told my people about having nothing to do with the Devil's Children. You tell your friends the same. If I see one of those brown skins down this side of the bad wires I'll tear him apart, man, woman or child. Joint by joint I'll tear him."

There was no point in arguing, so Nicky walked out into the midmorning glare and ran down the street, left through the Borough and up the lane to where Kewal was waiting for her in the shadow of the hedge. (Now that the job was known to be safe he had volunteered for it because it was also known to be easy.) He was almost as interested by the description of the court as Uncle Chacha had been by the first meeting with the giant.

"Yes," he said. "He is becoming a feudal baron, and he is setting about it the right way. It would be curious to know whether he has thought it out or whether his behavior is instinctive. The first step is to make all the villagers obey him, and this he must do partly by frequent demonstrations of his physical strength—that was why he broke the fork—and partly by laying down strict rules which they *can* obey. And at the same time he must channel all the business of the village through his own hands. Now a man who wants a fork mended or a scythe made must come to him, and if that man is out of favor with him then the work will not be done. So our forge is another source of power for him."

"He protects them too, don't forget," said Nicky. "And I thought they seemed to like being bullied like that, in a funny way."

"Oh yes, of course. Most people prefer to have their thinking done for them. Democracy is not a natural growth, it is a weary responsibility. You have to be sterling fellows, such as we Sikhs are, to make it work."

That afternoon two barrow loads of broken implements waited where the power lines crossed the lane. Uncle Jagindar and his assistants toiled in the roaring and clanging smithy as long as there was light. By Friday the work was done.

The giant scrutinized tool after tool in the Borough before handing them back to their owners, but as far as Nicky could tell from the blue, unwinking eyes and the blubbery cheeks he was satisfied. She explained about the pieces which Uncle Jagindar had said were past mending, and he nodded. Half an hour later she was herding two fat lambs up the lane, while a disgruntled Kewal toiled behind her shoving a barrow piled high with vegetables.

Chapter 5

LOST BOY

The sheep meant more work—hurdles to be woven from thin-sliced strips of chestnut wood, posts to be rammed into the ground to hold the hurdles steady in sheep-proof fences around an area where the hay had been cut. Then the fences had to be moved every two days to allow the flock to get at fresh grass. And men had to sleep out at the sheepfold all night to scare away wild dogs and foxes. The flock grew to about thirty animals by the end of August, so steadily did the smithy work; in fact Nicky and Kewal decided that the giant must be extending his empire by trading in metalwork with villages on the far side of Felpham, so many broken tools did he seem to find, so many orders for scythes and plowshares and horse harness were left each week with the barrows.

Nicky asked the giant one day if he could pay for the next big load with a horse, but he stared at her angrily and shook his head.

"I hear as they're carrying swords now," he purred suspiciously; the huge hand crept to the pommel of his cutlass.

"Yes," said Nicky. "It's part of their religion. They were soldiers ages ago, and they've always carried swords. My friends used to wear a little toy sword before . . . before . . . you know; now they've made themselves proper ones again, in case they have to fight somebody."

"And now they're wanting horses too," said the giant. Suddenly Nicky saw what was worrying him.

"But they don't want horses for fighting on," she said. "They don't want to fight anybody. They'd like horses for plowing and pulling carts and so on."

"That's as may be," said the giant. "But I'm not sparing any horses. I've given you a fair price for the work so far, haven't I?"

"Oh yes," said Nicky, and looked at a crate of baffled hens which was balanced across one of the barrows. "The Sikhs are very pleased."

"And so they ought to be," said the giant. "Well, if

they're making swords for themselves, they can make 'em for me too."

"I'll ask," said Nicky doubtfully.

"You do that," said the giant, and sauntered down the hill. He moved nowadays with a slow and lordly gait which seemed to imply that all the wide landscape belonged to him, and every creature in it.

But Uncle Jagindar refused to make weapons for anybody except his own people, and the Sikh council (though they argued the question around for twenty minutes) all agreed with him. When he heard the news the giant became surlier than ever with Nicky, and the villagers copied him. Partly, Nicky decided, this was because they just did whatever *he* did out of sheer awe for him; but it was also partly because of the way they had built up a whole network of myths and imaginings around the Sikhs. One or two things that Maxie said, or that Mr. Tom said when he was talking over smithwork to be done, showed that their heads were full of crazy notions. They stopped looking her in the face when they spoke to her, as though they were afraid of some power that might rest in her eye. Also, if there were children in the Borough when she came past, mothers' voices would yell a warning and little legs would scuttle for doorways. Once Nicky even saw a soapy arm reach through a window and grab a baby by the leg from where it was sleeping in a sort of wooden pram.

The giant still looked her straight in the eye, and

raged in his purring voice if he heard anyone suggest or hint that the Devil's Children were other than human flesh, but the scary whisperings went on behind his back. Nicky first realized how strong these dotty beliefs had become when she found the lost boy.

August had been a furiously busy month. The smithy furnace still roared all day, eating charcoal by the sackful. Ajeet and Nicky were officially in charge of the chickens, but that didn't excuse them from any other work that needed doing—looking after babies, or chasing escaped sheep, or dreary milling, or binding and stooking the untidy sheaves as the first wheat was reaped, and there were six scythes now to do the reaping. And then, a few days later, the dried sheaves were carried down to the lane and spread about for threshing; and that was woman's work, though after twenty minutes' drubbing at the gold mass with the clumsy threshing flail your neck and shoulders ached with sharp pain and your hands were all blisters.

But even threshing was better than plowing, which Mr. Surbans Singh insisted on making an experimental start on as soon as the sheaves were off the stubble.

"We're learning new sums," whispered Ajeet. "Four children equal one horse."

Nicky only grunted. She was trudging with six-inch steps through the shin-scratching stalks, leaning her weight right forward against the rope that led over the pad on her shoulder and back to the plow frame. Ajeet trudged beside her with another rope, and Gopal and his cousin Harpit just ahead; behind her Mr. Surbans Singh wrestled with the bucking plow handles as the blade surged in jolts and rushes through roots and flinty earth. It was very slow, very tiring, and turned only a wiggling, shallow furrow. When at last Mr. Surbans Singh called a halt, all four children sank groaning to the bristly stubble and watched while Mr. Surbans Singh and Uncle Jagindar and Mr. Wazir Singh (who had once been a farmer) scuffed at the turned earth with their feet, bent to trickle it through their fingers, and discussed the tilt and angle of the blade.

"Not bad," said Mr. Surbans Singh at last. "We cannot plow all these acres. The next thing is to take sharp poles and search for the best patches of earth."

"You can run away and play now, children," said Mr. Wazir Singh, who was one of those people who always manage to talk to children as though they are small and stupid and anything they do, even when they've been helping for all they're worth, is of no interest or importance.

"Thank you, Nicky," said Mr. Surbans Singh with his brilliant smile. She could see where broad streams of sweat had runneled through the dust on his face, and realized that he must have been toiling twice as hard as any of them.

"Thank you, Ajeet and Gopal and Harpit," he went

on. "Ask your aunt Mohindar to give you each an apple."

The apples in the artist's cottage garden weren't ready for eating yet, but the village had paid for some of the last lot of work with a sack of James Grieves. The children sat on the wall around the well and bit into the white flesh, so juicy that there was no way of stopping the sweet liquid flowing down the outside of their chins in wasteful dribbles. Nicky looked over the wide gold landscape, where the swifts hurtled and wheeled above wheat that would never be harvested, and felt the wanderlust on her. Suddenly the close community, busy with its ceaseless effort for survival, seemed stifling.

Usually she would have gone for rest and calm to sit by the old lady's cart under the wych elm and watch the babies playing. Even when Ajeet came to translate, she and the old lady did not speak much, though sometimes the old lady would tell her of extraordinary things she had seen and done in that other life before she came to England—not really as though she was trying to entertain Nicky, more to teach her, to instruct, to pass on precious knowledge. And when they didn't speak, it still was soothing to be near her, in a way that Nicky couldn't explain; she guessed that the old lady felt the same, but there was no way of asking.

But today the old lady had one of her little illnesses and had stayed in bed, not wanting to see anybody except her daughters, and then only to complain to them about something. So now Nicky longed to be out of earshot of the clang of the forge and the thud of the flails, away from the pricking and clotting dust which all this hard work stirred into the air, somewhere else.

"I'm going for a walk," she said as she threw her core away.

Harpit groaned. Gopal sighed.

"So I shall have to come with you," he said, "to slaughter your enemies."

He patted the three-quarter-size sword that swung against his hip. He was very proud of it because Uncle Jagindar said it was the best blade he'd made. One corner of the forge held a pile of snapped blades which hadn't stood up to the cruel testing the smiths gave them. ("What use is a sword," Uncle Chacha had asked, "if you strike with it once and then there is nothing left in your hand but the hilt?") Gopal joined the adults for fencing practice these days.

Now he patted his sword like a warrior and stood up.

"I'm afraid I haven't got any enemies for you," said Nicky as she stood too.

"Not even the bad baron?" said Harpit. That was what the children called the giant down in the village. It was funny to think that Nicky was the only one who'd ever seen him.

"No, he's not my enemy," said Nicky. "He's all right —in fact he's a hero, sort of."

"I must tell my mother where we're going," whispered Ajeet.

"I'll tell her," said Harpit, "and that means I needn't come on this idiot expedition. Where are you going, Nicky?"

"Up to the common."

Despite Gopal's sword, Nicky was the one who led the way down the curving line of elms and oaks that had been allowed to stay on the boundary between one farm and the next; the ripe barley brushed against their left shoulders; they dipped into the place where the line of trees became a farm track, whose slope took them down to join a magical and haunted lane, untarred, running nearly fifteen feet below the level of the surrounding fields. The hedge trees at the top of the banks on either side met far above their heads, so that the children walked in a cool green silence and looked up into the caverns where the earth had been washed away from between blanched tree roots. In that convenient dark the animals of the night laired. It was a street of foxes.

Then, too soon, they were out into the broad evening sun and turning left up the grassy track to the common. Swayne's farm, deserted now, stood silent on the corner—mainly a long wall of windowless brick, with gates opening into yards where cattle had once mooched and scuffled. Gopal, driven by some impulse to assert himself against the brooding stillness, drew the gray curved blade from his belt and lunged at imaginary foes; with each lunge he gave a grunting cry. The echo bounced off the brick wall on the far side of the farmyard, and died into stillness.

"Please stop it," said Ajeet. Gopal sheathed his sword, grinning.

The echo continued. It said "Help!"

Nicky climbed the gate into the farmyard. The dry litter rustled under her feet.

"Where are you?" she called.

"Here," said the faint voice. "Help! I'm stuck!"

They found him in the loft over a hay barn. A ladder lay on the floor of the barn, and in the square black hole in the ceiling a wan face floated. Nicky and Gopal lifted the fallen ladder back into place.

"I can't climb down," said the face. "I've hurt my foot." It began to sob.

"I'll come up and help you," said Gopal. "Don't worry. It's all right."

"Not you!" wailed the face. "I've got a brick. I'll hit you!"

Gopal took his hand off the rung and shrugged.

Nicky climbed slowly up the ladder. The face shifted in the square, and in the dimness behind she saw an arm move upward. She stopped climbing.

"It's quite all right," she said. "I won't hurt you. My name's Nicky Gore. What's yours?"

"Shan't tell you."

The arm with the brick wavered uncertainly. Nicky flinched.

"Look," she said, "if I'd got magic, your brick wouldn't hurt me, but if I haven't got magic, then you'd be hurting somebody just like yourself, somebody who's trying to help you."

"What about him?" said the boy, still panting with sobs.

"He wants to help you too. His name's Gopal. He's my friend. And the other one's Ajeet—she tells wonderful stories."

"Tell 'em to go away."

Nicky looked over her shoulder. Ajeet was already floating out like a shadow. Gopal shrugged again, tested the bottom of the ladder, and went to the door.

"Be careful," he said. "I *think* it's steady, but not if you start fighting on it."

Nicky managed a sort of laugh as she climbed into the darkness.

"How long have you been here?" she said.

"I been here all day. I was looking for treasure. There's a heap of treasure buried up on the common, folk say, but when I come to the farm I thought the farm folk might have found some, so I started looking here, and then I knocked the ladder down, and then I trod on a bit o' glass and it come clean through my foot. . . ."

He was about eight, very dirty, the dirt on his face all streaked with blubbering.

"Wriggle it around over the hole," said Nicky, "and I'll have a look."

He did so, with slow care; his groans sounded like acting, but the foot really did look horrid; the worn sneaker was covered with dried blood and the foot seemed to bulge unnaturally inside the canvas. The laces were taut and too knotted to undo, so Nicky drew her hunting knife (which Uncle Chacha had honed for her to a desperate sharpness) and sliced them delicately through. The boy cried aloud as the pressure altered, then sat sobbing. Nicky realized that she'd probably done the wrong thing. They must get him to an adult as soon as possible.

"Look," she said, "if I go down the ladder the wrong way around, then you can get yourself further over the hole, and I'll come back up until you're sitting on my shoulders. Then I can give you a piggyback down."

The boy nodded dully. Nicky stepped onto the ladder and went down until her head was below floor level. There she turned so that her heels were on the rungs.

"Now," she said, "see if you can wriggle your bottom along until your good leg is right over this side. A bit further. Now I'm coming up a rung. I'll hold your bad leg so that it doesn't bang anything."

"It hurts frightful when I drop it," groaned the boy.

"All right, I'll hold it up. Now you take hold of the ladder, lean forward against my head, and see if you can lift your bottom across so that you're sitting on the rung. Well done! Now let yourself slide down onto my shoulders; hold on to my forehead. Higher, you're covering my eyes. Hold tight. Down we go!"

The ladder creaked beneath the double weight. Nicky moved one heel carefully to the next rung, bending her knee out steadily so as to lower the two of them without a jolt. The wounded foot came through the opening with an inch to spare. Each rung seemed to take ages, as the thigh muscles above her bending knee were stretched to aching iron. She'd done five and was resting for the next when the grip on her forehead suddenly gave way.

"Hold tight!" she cried, and flung up her hand from the ladder to catch the slipping arm.

"Are you all right?" she said.

There was no answer. The boy's weight was now quite limp. Fresh blood was seeping, bright scarlet, through the crackled dark rind of the blood which had dried on his shoe before. Gopal, who must have been watching through the doorway, ran in and held the bottom of the ladder. She came down the last few rungs in one rush, trying to hold the boy from falling by forcing the back of her head into his stomach to slide him down the rungs. The top of the ladder bounced and rattled in the trapdoor, but stayed put.

"I've got his shoulders," said Gopal. "We've found something to carry him on outside. Can you manage?"

Nicky staggered out into the sunlight and saw Ajeet spreading hay onto a hurdle.

"This end," said Gopal. "Turn your back to it. Now get down as low as you can and I'll lift him off."

Nicky crouched, then sat; she twisted to ease the wounded leg onto the hay, and at last stood, shuddering with the long effort and feeling such sudden lightness that a breeze could have blown her away.

"Well done, Nicky," said Gopal. "Lift his leg, Ajeet, while I put more hay under it. If we get it higher than the body it might bleed a bit less. And then we'll need to lash it into place, so that it doesn't flop about while we are carrying him. A rope or a strap."

"No," said Ajeet, "something softer. What about your puggri?"

"It's such a bind to do up again," said Gopal, but he began to unwind the long folds of his turban. His black hair fell over his shoulders, like a girl's, but he twisted it up with a few practiced flicks and pinned it into place with the square wooden comb. The cloth was long enough to go three times around the hurdle, lashing the leg comfortably firm. The child muttered and stirred, but did not wake. His face looked a nasty yellowy gray beneath the tear-streaked dirt.

"Where shall we take him?" said Nicky.

"Up to the farm," said Gopal.

"He won't like that," said Nicky. "Nor will the villagers. They'll think we've stolen his soul away, or something."

"Never mind," said Gopal. "First, we don't know which house he belongs at, or even which village. Second, he must have proper medical attention, and he won't get *that* in the village."

"All right," said Nicky.

Gopal took the front of the hurdle, Nicky and Ajeet the two back corners. The first stretch along the deep lane was manageable, but after that it became harder even than plowing, and they had to rest every fifty yards. They were battling up through the barley field when a voice hissed at them from the trees. They all stopped and looked into the shadow, too tired to be frightened.

It was the risaldar, statuesque with his long bow, waiting for a rabbit or a pheasant. Obviously he was cross that they had spoilt his hunting, but after a question or two in Punjabi, answered by Gopal, he stepped out from his cover, handed the bow to Nicky, and took the girls' end of the hurdle. For the rest of the journey the children worked shift and shift on the front corners.

The communal supper was being carried out of the artist's cottage when they at last settled the hurdle wearily across the wellhead. The usual cackle of argument rose as the women gathered around the wounded boy, while the steam from the big bowls of curry rose pungent through the evening air. But Cousin Punam shushed the cooks away and had the hurdle carried into one of the sheds beside the farmyard.

"We will take the sock and shoe off while he's still fainted," she said, snipping busily with a pair of nail scissors. "Then he will never know how much it hurts, eh? I did not think, when I was doing my training, that so soon I would have to be a qualified doctor. A little boiled water, a little disinfectant, cotton wool . . . Ai, but that's a nasty cut! Pull very gently at this bit of sock, Nicky, while I cut here. Ah, how dirty! That's it, good—throw it straight on the fire. And don't come back for five minutes, Nicky, because now I must do something you will not like."

It was still more than an hour till nightfall. The last gold of sunset lay slant across the fields and in it the swifts still wheeled, hundreds of feet up, too high for her to hear their bloodless screaming. It was going to be another blazing day tomorrow, just right for the dreary toil of reaping and threshing. She leaned against the cottage wall and looked down at the square brick tower of the church, warm in that warm light. What next? The boy would be in trouble in the village if they learned he had crossed the bad wires; if the Sikhs simply put him on the hurdle and carried him down to the Borough, they could expect more suspicion than gratitude—and Cousin Punam *had* been going to do something "wrong" to him . . . Nicky would have to remind her to tie the wound up with a clean rag, and not anything out of her bag. . . .

Cousin Punam had finished, but was talking to someone. Nicky heard the words ". . . tetanus injection . . ." before she called out to ask whether she could come in. Neena was sponging the grime off the sleeping face.

"When will he wake up?" said Nicky.

"Quite soon, perhaps," said Cousin Punam.

"It sounds awful," said Nicky, "but he'll be terrified if he sees you. Let me wait, and I'll find out where he lives. Then we can take him back."

Cousin Punam sighed and shrugged, just as Gopal had done down at Swayne's.

"Have you had your supper, Nicky?" said Neena.

"Not yet."

"I'll send you some."

"Thank you," said Nicky. "And thank you, Punam, for . . . for everything."

She stumbled over the words, half conscious that she was speaking for the boy and his mother and the whole village words that they would never learn to say. The women left. Ajeet came back with a chapati—the heavy, sconelike bread which the Sikhs made—and mutton curry. Nicky was just learning to like the taste now that the Sikhs were beginning to run out of curry powder.

Perhaps it was the smell of food which woke the boy, because he tried to sit up when Ajeet was hardly out of the stall. Nicky rose from the floor, her mouth crammed with bread and curry.

"Don't try to move," she mumbled. "How does your leg feel?"

He looked at it as though he'd forgotten how it hurt, then at her, then, wide-eyed, around the dim unfamiliar stall.

"Where's the rest of them?" he whispered.

"Having their supper. You're all right. We'll look after you."

"I'm not telling you my name," he whispered fiercely. "My mum says don't you tell 'em your name if they catch you, and they've got no power on you, 'cause they don't know what to call you in their spells."

"If you'll tell me where you live, we'll carry you home as soon as it's dark."

"Oh," he said with a note of surprise.

"I thought we could say you'd been looking for birds' nests in that hedge below the bad wires, and one of us heard you calling and found you'd hurt your foot and brought you up here. Then nobody'd know you'd crossed the wires."

"Much too late for birds' nests," he said. "Where you come from, if you don't know that?"

"London," said Nicky. "Well, you think of something you might have been looking for at this time of year."

"Too early for crab apples or nuts," said the boy.

"Tell you what: I could have been looking for a rabbit run to put a snare in."

"That'll do," said Nicky, thinking that she ought to tell the risaldar about rabbit snares. "Do you live in the village, or outside it?"

"Right agin the edge," he said. "You can cut across to our back garden through Mr. Banstead's paddock."

"Good," said Nicky. "We won't go till it's nearly dark. I'm afraid your mother will be worrying for you."

"That she will," said the boy.

"Are you hungry?"

Suspicion tightened the lines of his face again.

"I'm not eating the Queer Folk's food," he muttered.

"I could bring you water from the well," Nicky suggested. "That was here before us. And there's a bag of apples which came up from the village only yesterday morning."

He thought for a few seconds, hunger and terror fighting.

"All right," he said at last.

After supper they lifted him gently back onto his hurdle and four of the uncles carried him down the lane. He stared at his bearers in mute fear until, between step and step, he fell deep asleep. Nicky had to shake him awake at the edge of the village so that he could tell them their way through the dusk.

It was the last cottage in the lane to Halling Down.

The uncles lowered the hurdle onto the dewy grass and stole off into the darkness by the paddock hedge. A dog yelped in the cottage next door as Nicky pushed the sagging gate open. A man's voice shouted at the dog. The door at the end of the path opened, sending faint gold across a cabbage patch. A woman stood in the rectangle of light. Nicky walked up the path.

"That you, Mike?" called the woman.

The boy cried faintly to her from his hurdle.

"I found him hurt," said Nicky, "so we bandaged him up and brought him home."

The woman picked up her long skirt and rushed down the path. It was the same Mrs. Sallow who'd been complaining in court about her neighbor's dog. When Nicky got back to the paddock she was kneeling by the stretcher with her arm under the boy's shoulders.

"His foot's very bad," said Nicky. "I think I could manage one end if you do the other."

Mrs. Sallow stood up and looked despairingly around. Obviously her feud with the dog owner meant she could expect no help from there, and she had no neighbor on the other side.

"All right," she said. "But mind you, I owe you nothing."

"Of course not," said Nicky.

The boy and the hurdle weighed like death. The boy groaned as they tilted through the gateway. The woman said nothing. Nicky lowered her end on the path outside the door.

"I'll cope from here," said the woman. She knelt by the hurdle and pulled the boy to her. Then with a painful effort she staggered to her feet. Nicky held the door open for her.

"You keep out," said the woman.

"I never told 'em my name, Mum," said the boy.

"Good lad," said the woman.

"But, Mum . . ." said the boy.

"Tell me later," she said, and kicked the door shut with her heel.

Nicky had dragged the hurdle down the path and joined the uncles by the hedge when the cottage door opened again. Mrs. Sallow stood in the doorway, hands on her hips, head thrown back.

"You people," she called. "I give you my thanks for what you have done for my boy."

The door shut as the neighbor's dog exploded into an ecstasy of yelping.

"What was the significance of that?" said Mr. Surbans Singh.

"It's unlucky to take help from fairies," explained Nicky, "if you don't thank them. All the stories say so. Goodness I'm tired."

"In that case," said Mr. Surbans Singh, "it is most fortunate that we happen to have a magic hurdle here, with four demons to carry it."

So Nicky rode home through the dark while the uncles made low-voiced jokes about their supernatural powers. It was almost a month before she saw Mike Sallow again.

Chapter 6

THIEVES' HARVEST

They had been plowing all day, with four plows going and every man and woman, as well as all the older children, taking turns at the heavy chore. Between turns they worked at the two strips which were wanted for autumn sowing, breaking down the clods with hoes and dragging the harrow to and fro to produce a fine tilth. The thin strips of turned earth looked pitiful amid the rolling steppes of stubble and unmown wheat. The strips were scattered apparently at random over the farm, wherever prodding with sticks had shown the soil to be deepest or least flinty, or where there seemed some promise of shelter from the winds. There'd been no rain for a week, so the soil was light and workable, which was why the whole community was slaving at it today. On other days logging parties had been up in the woods, getting in fuel for the winter. And twice a raiding party had set off at dusk, trekked the twenty miles to Reading through the safe night, stayed in the empty city all day, and trekked back laden with stores and blocks of the most precious stuff in all England, salt.

But today had been stolid plowing. Resting between her turns, Nicky had been vaguely conscious that something was happening down in the village. The bells rang for a minute, not their proper changes, and then stopped. Shouts drifted up against the breeze, but so faint and far that she didn't piece them together into a coherent sequence, or even realize that they were more and louder than they might have been.

About six it was time to go and get the hens in by scattering corn in their coops. If you left it later than that they tried to roost out in the shrubs of the farmhouse garden. She was helping Ajeet search the tattered lavender bushes for hidden nests when she saw, down the lane and out of the corner of her eye, a furtive movement—somebody ducking into the crook of the bank to avoid being seen. Kewal, she thought, out checking the rabbit snares to escape his share of plowing. But Kewal had been up in the field, lugging at the ropes as steadily as anyone (it was really only that he didn't like *starting* jobs) and besides, hadn't the shape in the lane had fair hair? And wasn't there something awkward about the way it had moved?

Inquisitive, she slid down the bank and stole along the lane. They all went barefooted as often as possible now, because shoes were wearing out and making new ones was a job for winter evenings. No council workmen had been along the lanes of England that summer, keeping the verges trim, so you could bury yourself deep in the rank grasses. Mike, peering between the stems, must have seen her coming; but he stayed where he was. He had been crying, but now his mouth was working down and sideways as though something sticky had lodged in the corner of his jaw; his lungs pumped in dry, jerking spasms.

"What's the matter, Mike?" said Nicky, forgetting that she wasn't supposed to know his name. But he'd forgotten too.

"The robbers have come!" he gasped. "The robbers have come!"

Nicky stared at him, not taking it in.

"They was herding all the children together," said Mike, "and taking 'em off somewheres. I was abed still, with my foot, but my mum shoved me out of the back gate and says to come to you. I been crawling across the fields, but I dursn't come no further, though you done me good once. My mum says you done my foot good."

"But what about Mr. Barnard—the Master? Didn't he stop them?"

"They killed him! They killed him!"

Mike began to wail, and Nicky's whole being was flooded by a chill of shock at the thought of that huge life murdered. She put her arm around Mike's shoulders and waited for the sobbing to stop.

"Come with me," she said. "My friends will know what to do. Shall I give you a piggyback again?"

"I'll do," sniffled the boy. "There's not nowhere else to go, is there?"

"That's right," said Nicky, and helped him, half hobbling and half hopping, up the lane. His foot was still clearly very sore, and she could see from his scrattled knees that he really must have crawled most of the way.

Ajeet was standing in the lane with the basket of eggs. The boy flinched when he saw her, but came on.

"Come and help me talk to your grandmother," said Nicky. "Robbers have come to the village and killed the big man. They're taking all the children somewhere, Mike says—as hostages, I suppose. That means they're going to stay."

Ajeet never looked as though anything had surprised her. Now she just nodded her small head and walked up to the wych elm where the old lady held court on fine days. The big tree stood right against the lane above the farmyard and here in a flattened and dusty area of what had been barley field the small children scuffled and dug, while the old lady lay on her cushions in the shade and gave orders to everything that came in sight, or

gathered her grandchildren and great-grandchildren
into a ring and told them long, marvelous fairy tales.
One of the mothers was always there to do the donkey
work of the nursery, but the old lady was its genius.

By the time Nicky had brought Mike hobbling up and
settled him in comfort in the dust, Ajeet had told the
news. Nicky turned toward the tree, put her palms together under her chin and bowed. The old lady did the
same on her cushions, just as if Nicky were an important
person come from many miles away to visit her. The old
lady rattled a sharp sentence at the children who'd
gathered to listen, and they scattered.

Ajeet said, "My grandmother wants the boy to tell his
story again."

Mike was staring at the old lady with quivering lips.
Nicky remembered how terrified *she'd* been when she
first faced those brilliant eyes.

"He told me that robbers had come to the village,"
she said. "They'd started herding the children together
and taking them somewhere. He was in bed with his bad
foot, and his mother smuggled him out of the back door
and told him to come to us. He said the robbers had
killed the big man. Do you know any more, Mike?"

"My mum said they was on horses, in armor," he
whispered.

Ajeet translated. Mike couldn't remember any more.
He'd seen nothing himself, though he'd heard the cries

from his bed, and the church bell ringing its alarm and then stopping.

The old lady spoke to Tara Deep, the mother who'd been looking after the nursery. She nodded and began to walk up to the plowmen, quick and graceful in her blue sari. The old lady spoke directly to Nicky.

"My grandmother wants to know what *you* think we should do," said Ajeet.

"First we've got to make ourselves as safe as we can," said Nicky, "and then we've got to find out more, how many of them there are, and what they're going to do next. We can't decide anything until we get more news. The only thing is, the robbers won't mind crossing the bad wires—they must have passed things just as bad to get to the village at all."

"I just shuts my eyes and ducks under," said Mike.

"The farmyard's almost a fort already," said Nicky. "We could get food and water in, and the sheep, and strengthen it. And as soon as it's dark I'll go down across the fields and try and find somebody I know. Mr. Tom's house has its back to the school playground, and then there's a path and then fields, so I might be able to get to him without going through the village at all. After all, we aren't really sure that Mike's got his story right— his mother must have been very hurried and worried."

Ajeet had been translating as Nicky went along. The old lady raised a ringed hand, palm toward Nicky in a sort of salute, and answered. Ajeet laughed.

"My grandmother says you'll make a very good wife for a soldier someday," she said.

Nicky nodded, unsmiling. She was frightened, of course, by what she had suggested, but another part of her felt a strange, grim satisfaction in the risks and dangers. They would force her to rebuild the armor around her heart, which during the last few weeks she had allowed to become so full of chinks and weaknesses. She bowed her head and stared at the scuffled dust; at the thought of the coming action her heart began to hammer—as though there were a small smithy in there, retempering the rusted steel.

By now the men were trooping down from the field, talking excitedly and looking northeast across the swooping acres to where the church tower stood peaceful among its lindens. The women called their own children to them as they came, and cajoled them into stillness and silence. A big orderly circle gathered under the wych elm, the men stopped chattering and the old woman spoke. Nicky heard her own name jut out from the fuzz of Punjabi; heads turned toward her. Then, as usual, twenty voices broke into argument together; the old lady screeched, and Uncle Jagindar was talking alone. Voices grunted agreement. He turned to Nicky.

"This sounds dangerous," he said, "but we can send a guard with you."

"I don't think it's *very* dangerous," said Nicky. "If

they catch me, they'll think I'm one of the village children and put me with the others as a hostage. But I don't see why they should—they can't watch the whole village, all the way around. If you do send a guard, you won't have so many men for the defense up here, supposing they decided to attack tonight, which would be the sensible thing for them. It'd be a waste of our men. You'll need sentries all night, too."

She could see heads nodding.

"Perhaps Gopal could come with me," she said. "Not to fight or anything, but to bring back news if I do get caught. The thing is, I'm sure I'm the only person Mr. Tom or any of them would talk to, so it's no use any of you going. They're a bit scared of me, but not half so much as they are of you. That's right, isn't it, Mike?"

"Yes, that's right," he whispered, staring around at the dark and bearded faces.

"And we've got to *know*, haven't we?" she said. "We can't decide anything till then."

Uncle Jagindar wheeled to the ring of Sikhs.

"That is agreed, my friends?" he asked.

"Agreed," boomed the council.

He started to allot tasks in Punjabi. Gopal came, serious-faced, to Nicky.

"Our job is to eat and rest," he said. "Mike looks as if he needs a rest too."

The boy nodded, but they had to help him to his feet and support him, swaying, down to the farmyard. Already the water carriers were bringing bucket after bucket clanking from the well, while the carts creaked up from the farmhouse with larderfuls of dry stores and cans. Sacks of charcoal were carried in from the smithy, for cooking, and mounds of hay down from the big barn for the sheep. Soon the sheep themselves flooded, baaing with amazement, into the bustling square. The cooped hens were trundled up the lane; barrows of blankets and bedding came from the houses, sacks of new corn from the storage towers. The old lady was ensconced in an open stall, and the holy book carried reverently in from the bungalow.

As dusk fell the courtyard was still a shouting and baaing and cackling confusion. The communal supper was going to be very late, cooked on the faint-flamed and smokeless charcoal instead of the roaring logs they'd used when they first spent a night there. But Nicky had already eaten; her fair hair was covered with a dark scarf; she wore a navy blue jersey and a pair of dark gray trousers belonging to Gopal; she would have liked to blacken her face, but could imagine the effect on an already terrified Mr. Tom if a dark face hissed at him out of the night. His was obviously the first house to try.

After the clamor and reek and dust of the courtyard, the dewy air of nightfall would have seemed bliss to breathe if her heart hadn't been beating so fiercely. Gopal eased his sword in its scabbard, then frowned at the slight click. They stole down the familiar lane side by side. Mr. Kirpal Singh, crouched by a lone bush on the bank, whispered them good luck. (Five sentries watching for two hours each: everyone was going to be very tired tomorrow.)

There was a copse on the right of the lane below the bad wires. They headed south beside it, and on up the slope under the cover of a hedge which had not been hauled out because it marked the boundary between two farms. After two hundred yards they turned east again, leaving the hedge to slip like hunting stoats along the edge of a stand of barley. There was no hurry. The night was still dark gray, and Nicky didn't want to reach the playing field until it was fully black. So where the barley stopped, because that was as far as the reapers had mown, they lay on their stomachs, trying to suck the last inch of seeing out of the shortening distances, peering and listening for dangers. A lone pheasant clacked in a copse to their right.

"They can't post sentries all around a village as big as this," whispered Gopal. "Not unless there are hundreds of men. In any case they don't need to defend the whole village now they have hostages. They'll guard the place where they've set up camp, and then perhaps they'll send out patrols. That's what we must watch out for."

Beyond the reaped stubble was a pasture field where cows stumbled and snorted, invisible from twenty yards. Knowing what inquisitive brutes cows can be the children steered to the right, where an extra loom in the dark promised the shelter of another hedge. But when it came it was double, and a lane ran down the middle. Nicky shook her head—such a path was a likely route for a patrol. They scouted left, and the lane bent at right angles; flitting through a gap in the hedges, they found themselves once more at a place where unreaped wheat ran beside stubble, and ran in what Nicky, even after that bout of dodging, still thought was the right direction. Then another lane to cross, and empty pasture beyond. It was too dark to see more than ten yards now.

After a whispered talk, Gopal dropped behind and Nicky tucked a white rag into her belt for him to follow her by, like the scut of a rabbit. (If they were chased, she'd have to remember to snatch it out.) Darkness made the middle of fields seem safer than hedges; but coming in darkness to the village, by this unfamiliar way, she might easily have missed her direction. The wind had been steady from the southwest all day, surely. Just as she decided to stop and reconsider, the church clock began to clang sweetly to her left. Eight. More to her front, but further away, urgent voices yelled. In the fresh silence the tussocky grass of the pasture seemed to swish horribly loudly, however carefully she moved her feet; anyone waiting in the coming hedge would be bound to hear her—though she couldn't hear Gopal ten paces behind her. Encouraged, she stole forward.

This hedge was double too, but the path down the middle was only a yard across. So she knew where she was, at least; this was the footpath that ran south between the church and the school. The nearer hedge was strengthened with the thorny wire she hated so much. As she squatted and wondered whether there'd be a gap further along, Gopal edged quietly up beside her.

"Barbed wire?" he whispered. "Wait a moment."

He crouched by the fence, holding some sort of tool in his hand. Two clicks, and he dragged a strand of wire away.

"My own idea," he whispered. "Wire cutters. You can crawl through now. Is it far from here?"

"Only across the playing field."

"Then tie your rag to the other hedge so that we can find the place coming back."

Most of the householders in the council estate kept a dog, but Mr. Tom preferred his scarred old tabby; so if they came up straight behind the right house there oughtn't to be any barking. Nicky lay in the dewy grass and tried to make out the roof lines; Mrs. Bower's chimney, next door, had a big hunched cowl. So . . .

Only firelight showed through Mr. Tom's parlor window. Nicky edged an eye above the sill, hoping that he hadn't gone to bed yet. No. He was curled in a chair by the dying fire, his head in his hands but held so low that it was almost on his knees; he looked very old and beaten. Nicky tapped cautiously on the pane. At the third tap he looked over his shoulder like a haunted man, and then put his head back between his hands. She kept on tapping, in a steady double rhythm which couldn't have been caused by anything accidental, such as a flying beetle. At last he staggered from the chair, crossed the room and opened the window half an inch.

"Who's there?" he whispered.

"Me. The girl from Booker's Farm. I want to talk to you."

"I'll have nothing to do with you," he hissed, and tried to shut the window. But Nicky was ready for him and jammed the hilt of her knife into the crack.

"We want to help you," she whispered. "But we can't until we know what's happening."

"How many o' you's out there, then?"

"Only me and a boy. He'll rap on the window if he hears anyone coming."

"Okay," said Mr. Tom after a pause. "I'll let you in."

"I'll climb through the window," said Nicky. He opened it wide and she flicked herself through. The moment she was in he fastened it tight, while Nicky tucked herself into a corner where she couldn't be seen from outside.

"Sit like you were sitting before," she suggested. "Talk as though you were talking to yourself. Mike Sallow came up to the farm and told us that robbers had come to the village and killed Mr. Barnard and taken all the children somewhere."

"True enough," groaned Mr. Tom. "They killed the Master. I was there, waiting for the fun of seeing him drive 'em off, but there was three of them on horses, wearing armor. They charged him down and skewered him through and through, so's he never got not one blow in with that sword of his. And then they cut his head off and stuck it on the pole of the Five Bells, for the wide world to see what manner of men they are. And herded all the children together, all as they could find, and took 'em down to a barn behind White House; and they put 'em in a loft with a pile of hay and timber down below, and they made old Maxie cry through the streets that they'll set fire to the whole shoot if they have a mite more trouble out of us during their stay."

"How long will that be?" said Nicky.

"As long as there's a morsel left to eat, that's my guess. And the Master was that set on us coming through the winter short of starving that we've barnfuls of stores waiting. You mark my words, we'll have 'em for months yet."

"How many of them are there?"

"Thirty. Maybe thirty-five."

"But there must be more than a hundred men in the village!"

"I know what you're thinking, girl, but they fell on us that sudden, and we had't nothing to fight 'em with, save a few cudgels. The Master, he'd been set on getting us swords, so he could have his own little army, but your folk wouldn't make 'em for us, remember? And these robbers come with spears, and horsemen in armor, and now they've got the children—though I've none of my own, thank God—and we're bound hand and foot, hand and foot."

"Do you think they'd actually burn the children if there was trouble?"

"I don't know, a course; but I do know they'd do *something,* and something pretty cruel, too. There was one of 'em, one of the ones on horseback, and while the footmen were hacking off the Master's head I saw him throw back his helmet to wipe his face. Curly hair, he had, and a broken nose, though he was scarce more than a boy. And when he saw Arthur's head dripping up there on the pole, he laughed like a lover. Like a lover in spring. I slunk away and come back here, and the rest I know from Maxie's crying."

He had been half out of his chair, glaring around the room as he tried to tell her the horror of his story, but a faint rap on the window made him shrink and curl like a snail. Nicky made a dart for the window, heard the footsteps, knew it was too late and slid herself under an old Put-U-Up bed where she lay, barely breathing, against the wall. A hard fist thundered at the front door. She could see Mr. Tom's feet rise from the floor, as though he were trying to curl himself even further into his chair.

"Go and answer him," whispered Nicky. "It'll be worse if you don't."

The feet doddered back to the floor. The legs stumbled past the dying fire. Then a bolt was drawn, slap. Then voices.

"What's your name, gaffer?"

"T-t-tom Pritchard."

"Tom Pritchard, eh? Fetch us each a mug of ale, Tom Pritchard."

More than one of them, then.

Shufflings, another door moving, palsied clinking of glass, more shufflings. Silence. Then the smash and tinkle of deliberately dropped tumblers.

"We hear you were a crony of the big man's, Tom Pritchard."

"N-n-no, not me. He broke my fork a-purpose."

"What d'you know about the lot they call the Devil's Children, Tom Pritchard? We hear as you had dealings with 'em."

"N-n-not much. They live up at Booker's, 'tother side of the bad wires. Three months back they came there. I had a bit of dealings with the girl as lives with them. She's an ordinary girl, to look at. The Master wouldn't have none of 'em but her in the village, and then only to do dealings in smithwork. They make and mend iron for us, they do, and sometimes I helped with the dealings. I never seen none of the others, saving the girl."

"Ah."

A low discussion.

"What are you doing still dressed this time o' night, Tom Pritchard? Thinking of going out, eh?"

"I . . . I couldn't sleep. I was sitting by the fire. I hadn't a light showing. I heard the orders."

"At least you ain't deaf, then, Tom Pritchard. Well, it's time good little gaffers were in bed, even them that can't sleep. I want to see you going up them stairs, Tom Pritchard. You can sleep now, gaffer. The Devil's Children needn't fright your dreams no more, not now we're here to look after you. We'll nip up there and sort 'em out for you, soon as we're settled. Up you go now, like a good gaffer."

A grunt, and the stumble and thud of Mr. Tom being shoved so hard along the hallway that he fell. Slow steps on the stairs. More talk at the porch, then footsteps coming, but turning off through the other door. A curse as something fell from a larder shelf. Voices in the hallway.

"Nice drop of ale they brew, leastways."

"Yeah. Cozy old spot to winter out. Scour around for more hosses, get them Devil's Children to run us up armor for the lot of us . . ."

"How'll you manage that, then?"

"Same as here. Devil's Children got children of their own, ain't they?"

Laughter.

"Be getting along then. Hey, Maxie, who's next?"

The crow of the clerk's voice from the street, shrill with terror.

"Sim Jenkins, sir."

Heels crunching through the broken tumblers on the doorstep. Going.

Nicky lay in the stillness and counted two thousand. She had an instinct that the robbers were the sort of people who would do the thing properly, when they wanted to scare a village into obedient terror. They wouldn't leave Mr. Tom quivering in the shameful dark without letting him know that they were still keeping an eye on him. And sure enough, when she was in the sixteen hundreds, another light tap came from the window. Thirty seconds later the front door slammed open, feet drummed on the stairs, more doors crashed and banged upstairs, and the hard voice shouted "Just come to tuck you up, gaffer. See that you *are* in bed, eh? Sweet dreams."

Feet on the stairs again, and the door walloping shut, and the crunched glass. Then the dreary business of starting once more at one, two, three . . .

She was so stiff when she edged the window open that she had to clamber through like an old woman. Halfway up the garden Gopal floated beside her from behind the runner beans; he touched her cheek with his hand in gentle welcome, then led the way back across the school playground to where the faint whiteness of their rag in the hedge marked the cut wires.

They took the journey home as carefully as they'd come, but nothing stopped or even scared them until their own sentry hissed at them out of his hiding and made their tired hearts bounce. Though it was well past midnight, every adult Sikh was awake and waiting in the dark farmyard. Nicky told her story in English, breaking it into short lengths so that Uncle Jagindar could turn it into Punjabi for the old lady. The pauses while he spoke enabled her to think, so that she left nothing out. When she had finished, five of the men crept out to relieve the sentries; for them she told the whole story all over again. Now every Sikh knew, and Nicky could sleep.

They held a council as soon as breakfast and the morning prayers were over. Daylight meant that Gopal and Harpit and the other children could stand sentry; from the upstairs windows of the farmhouse, from the hayrick in the big barn, from the upper branches of the wych elm, every scrap of country could be seen. The sheep were driven out to a new pen, close to the farmyard, but the hens were left to cluck and scrattle while the council talked. Nicky was there, with Ajeet to tell her what was said. Otherwise there was nobody younger than Kewal.

"Uncle Jagindar is asking if there is anyone who thinks we must move from here . . . they all say no . . . Mr. Kirpal Singh says we can either wait and defend ourselves if they attack us, or attack them before they are ready . . . Aunt Neena says they may not attack us . . . several people say they will . . . my grandmother is calling for quiet . . ."

"Nicky," said Uncle Jagindar, "you heard the men say they would not leave us alone, I think."

"Yes," said Nicky. "They told Mr. Tom that they were going to come and, er, 'sort you out' as soon as they were settled in the village. And they want you to make more armor for them. They were going to take the children as hostages."

The murmur of voices broke into fresh clamor. Ajeet sorted out what mattered.

"Mr. Wazir Singh says we could defend ourselves here forever. My father says no, not against thirty-five men with the only water on the other side of the road. My grandmother says the place would be a trap—a week, safe; a month, death. Mr. Wazir Singh says how can fifteen men attack thirty-five. And they have hostages, my mother says. Take them at dawn before they are ready, says Uncle Jagindar. Take the barn where the children are first, says the risaldar. Kill as many as we can in their beds, says my grandmother. My father says first we must watch them, to find out where the sentries are and what they do, especially at night. Scouts must go and watch, says Uncle Jagindar, but they must be careful not to be seen lest they put the robbers on their guard. Watch for two nights, strike on the third, says my grandmother. Mr. Surbans Singh says that meanwhile we must seem to be farming exactly as usual, but keep a secret watch out everywhere around the farm. They will send scouts up soon. Aunt Neena says that the children must stay near the farmyard. My grandmother tells me to tell you that the order includes you, Nicky . . ."

Nicky nodded, to show she had understood.

". . . now the risaldar says we must pretend to be felling wood for the winter, and cut the nearest trees in the row beyond the cottage so that they cannot creep up on us that way. And set fire to the barley, says my grandmother . . ."

"Nicky," said Uncle Jagindar, "is there anything more? You know the village and we do not."

"I think White House must be that very big one out on the far side, but I haven't seen it since we first came through. The other thing is the hostages. We've got to think of a plan to keep them safe. It's not just because they're children. If we attack the robbers and the robbers kill the children in revenge, then the village will come and massacre all of us. There's over a hundred men in Felpham, and once they really get angry . . ."

"You are right," said Uncle Chacha. "We must be quick and careful when the time comes. And we must be ready to run away if we fail."

The council shambled on, going over the same points several times, but slowly reaching the practical business of sentry duty and scout duty. At last they all dispersed to the tense charade of pretending to be innocent farmers while watching every hedge and hollow in case it should hide an ambush, and at the same time planning a murderous onslaught on an army more than twice their size. There was one false alarm that day: the enemy spy, sneaking up the line of trees in the dusk, turned out to be Mrs. Sallow, bedraggled and terrified but determined to know whether her son was safe. She sat in silence by Mike's straw, but after supper Nicky wheedled out of her some useful news of the robbers' arrangements.

Next day tempers were short with lack of sleep. The men took turns to rest, but some had to be on show for the benefit of the robber spies who lurked along the hillside; they thought they spotted three of these, but had to act as if they hadn't.

In the dark hour after the third midnight a whisper went around the farmyard. The women turned out with swords and spears to stand sentry, while the raiding party stole up the hill; fifteen grown men, and four lads. And Nicky. If the first phase of the attack succeeded, somebody would have to keep the rescued children from squealing panic, or the sleeping robbers would be woken and the second phase ruined. And that would have to be Nicky.

She thought she was the youngest of the long line creeping through the dark, until a hand took hers. It was Ajeet. None of the men noticed the extra child.

The wide loop around the village, taken at a stalker's

pace, with many pauses, lasted hours, but they were still too early.

In that first faint grayness when the birds begin to whistle in the copses, they struck.

Chapter 7

BLOOD ON THE SWORDS

Nicky lay on her stomach on the chill bank of a ditch; or perhaps it was the beginnings of a stream, for her legs were wet to the knee, despite the dry spell they'd been having. To left and right of her, like troops waiting to attack from a trench, was the tiny Sikh army. The blackness of night seemed no less than it had been, but now she could be sure of the hulk of the barn; the big house, over to her right, was still an undistinguishable mass of roof and treetops and outbuildings. She was rubbery cold, and thankful that the Sikhs (full of the sensible instincts of campaigning) had made her wear twice the clothes she'd thought she'd need.

In the dark ahead of her Uncle Chacha was stalking the sentry. Two of the robbers slept in the barn, taking turn and turn to watch outside while the other slept by a brazier. An oil-soaked torch was ready there, which the inside man could thrust into the brazier and bring to crackling life. Dry straw, dry hay, dry brushwood were heaped along the tarred timber of the walls; and there were two wicked cars there, whose tanks would explode if the fire blazed hot enough. The whole room was a bomb, and above it slept the children. (Mrs. Sallow had told them these details, because the robbers had shown the mothers of Felpham their precautions on the very first morning.) The Sikh scouts had studied the movements of the sentries; and the first thing was to catch the outside one just before the time for the last changeover. About now, in this dimness . . .

Only the nervy ears of the watchers in the ditch could have caught that faint thud. There was no cry. Shadows shifted to her left—Uncle Jagindar and the risaldar stealing forward. Three short raps and a long pause and two more short raps was the signal the sentries used. It had to be given two or three times, so that the man inside had time to know where he was—sleeping in a straw-filled barn by a brazier, with forty terrified children in the loft above.

The raps came loud as doom through the still, chill air. The watchers waited. Then the signal again. And

. . . but it was interrupted the third time by creaking hinges.

Now there was a cry, but faint—more of a gargling snort than any noise a man makes when he means something. But a meaning was there and Nicky shuddered in the ditch: there is only one sure way of keeping an enemy silent, the Sikhs had insisted, and that is to kill him. The hulk of the barn altered its shape: a big door swinging open, but no orange glow from fire beginning to gnaw into hay and timber. The army rose from its trench and crept toward the barn, Kewal and Gopal carrying plastic buckets filled from the ditch. In the doorway they met Uncle Jagindar and the risaldar carrying the brazier out on poles, while Uncle Chacha walked beside them holding a piece of tarpaulin to screen the light of it from any possible watcher in the house. Kewal and Gopal threw the water in their buckets across the piled hay and went back for more. The robbers had also kept buckets of water ready by the brazier (though they hadn't shown the Felpham women this precaution) and one of the uncles scattered their contents about.

Nicky felt her way up the steep stair and slid back the bolt of the door. The door rasped horribly as she edged it inward, and she looked down to see whether the noise had worried the Sikhs; but only Gopal and Ajeet stood in the grayness that came through the barn door. The others must already be stealing off across the unmown lawn toward the big house.

Inside the loft a child, children, began to wail. Nicky stood on the top step, gulping with rage at her own stupidity—she should never have climbed to the loft until a child stirred. But it was too late now. She pushed the door wide and stepped in.

The loft stank. Five windows gave real light. Dawn was coming fast. Sleeping children littered the moldy hay, in attitudes horribly like those of the two dead robbers on the grass outside the barn. But three were already woken to the nightmare day, and wailing. Nicky put her finger to her lips. The wailing stopped, but the wailers shrank from her as though she'd been a poisonous spider. More of them were stirring now—older ones.

"It's quite all right," said Nicky. "We've come to help you."

The words came out all strange and awkward. Nicky wasn't used to being hated and feared.

"Go away!" said a redheaded girl, about her own age.

More children were moving. A six-year-old boy sat suddenly bolt up, as though someone had pinched him; he stared at Nicky for five full seconds and began to screech. Some of them were standing now, but still cowering away from her. A babble like a playground rose—this was wrong, awful, dangerous. Everything depended on keeping the children quiet until the attack on the house had started.

"Shut up!" shouted Nicky, and stamped her foot.

There was a moment's silence, then the noise began to bubble up again, then it hushed. Ajeet walked past Nicky as though she wasn't there, right to the end of the stinking loft, turned, settled cross-legged onto a bale and held the whole room still with her dark, beautiful eyes. Just as the silence was beginning to crumble, she spoke.

"Be quiet, please," she said in a clear voice. "I am going to tell you a story. Will you all sit down please?"

Every child settled.

"There was a tiger once which had no soul," said Ajeet. "All day and all night it raged through the forest, seeking a soul which it could make its own. Now, in those forests there lived a woodman, and he had two sons . . ."

Her hands were moving already. The jungle grew at her fingertips, and through it the tiger stalked and roared, and the woodman's sons adventured. Nicky saw a child which had slept through the din wake slowly, sit up and start listening, as though this were how every morning of its life began. Terrified of breaking the spell, Nicky tiptoed to a window.

She could see the house clearly now; white and square, very big, with a low slate roof ending in a brim like a Chinese peasant's hat. Here a cheerful stockbroker had lived six months before; along these paths his children had larked or mooned as the mood took them; an old gardener had mown the big lawns smooth enough for croquet. And now they were all gone, and the lawns were lank, and murder crept across them. Any minute now . . .

A crash of glass, and a cry, and then a wild yelling. A naked white man was running across the lawn with a Sikh after him. The naked man ran faster and disappeared among trees, and the Sikh stopped and trotted back to the house. A cracked bell began a raucous clank —the alarm signal—but stopped before it had rung a dozen times. One, two, three, four men jumped from an upstairs window and ran to the largest of the outbuildings. From another window a figure flew, tumbling as he fell; when he hit the grass he lay still, and a second later Nicky heard the crash of the big pane through which he had been thrown. In the twanging silence that followed, Nicky studied the geography of the buildings and tried to plan for disaster. Suppose a sortie of robbers rushed from the house, would there be time to get the children down the stairs? The robbers had chosen the barn for their hostages because it was set nearly a hundred yards from the other buildings, and they could fire it without endangering themselves. Supposing the four men now cowering in the large outbuilding—just as far away across the paddock-like turf, but more to the left—plucked up their courage for revenge . . . A hoarse yell wavered across the grass, rising to a sharp scream, cut short.

Nicky looked over her shoulder to see how the children were taking these desperate noises. Should they leave now, and risk meeting a party of escaping robbers, or a returning patrol? No. Ajeet still held them enthralled: the woodman's second son was exchanging riddles with the tiger that had no soul. The tiger had already possessed the soul of the elder son, but needed a second man's soul to make up a whole tiger's soul. Nicky crossed the room and looked down the steep stair. Gopal had finished soaking the straw and was standing, watchful but relaxed, behind one doorpost. He had closed one leaf of the door. Nicky was on the point of going down to ask what he thought about moving the children when his stance tensed. She darted back to her window.

A man had led a huge horse from the outbuilding door. A strange figure moved beyond the animal and two other men came behind. The horse stopped. The two men went to the strange figure, bent out of sight and heaved.

The knight erupted into his saddle. He still looked strange, because his armor was so clumsy, but now he looked terrifying too—a giant toy which someone has put together from leftover bits of puppets and dolls, and then brought to gawky life. He put out his hand and a man passed him up his spear; a little crimson flag fluttered below the point. Now the man passed him a big timber ax and the knight hooked it into his belt, then turned and said something to the men. Two of them went back into the stables, but the third put a trumpet to his lips and blew a long, shivering note. The knight kicked his heels against the horse's ribs and the big animal started a slow trot over the lawn, toward the barn. Nicky heard the second leaf of the door creak shut, and the bar fall into place. The third man had followed the other two into the stables.

Beyond the knight a dark figure appeared from a downstairs window and stood for a moment, round as a bubble, against the whitewashed wall. Then Uncle Chacha was trotting across the grass, unhurriedly, as though he were slightly late for an appointment. Nicky could see the knight's face now, for the gawky helmet hung back over his shoulders and clanked dully as he bounced in his saddle. His hair was tight gold curls, his cheeks smooth; his nose was a ruin—broken in some old fight and mended all lopsided; below it his handsome mouth grinned cheerfully. As he came he fitted the lance into a holder, so that it stood up like a mast behind his thigh. Now he could wield his ax, two-handed.

Nicky looked around the room for something to throw, though none of the windows was near enough over the door; she might unsettle the horse for a minute, perhaps. But there seemed to be nothing in the loft except hay and children. She craned back out of the stench into the murderous sweet air.

The knight had ranged his horse alongside the door

and already the big ax was swung up over his shoulder
for a blow. His armor had gaps between the separate
pieces, to allow his limbs to move freely; really it was
only pieces of boiler and drainpipe held together with
straps.

He looked up to Nicky's window; his green mad eyes
caught and held hers; then he laughed, as Mr. Tom had
said, like a lover, and swung the ax. The blade crunched
through the half-rotted planking and he wrenched it
free and hefted it for another blow. Nicky didn't dare
look to where Uncle Chacha came trotting over the
sward; his best hope—his only hope—was to catch the
knight unawares and thrust through one of the joints of
his armor. Instead she looked toward the stable.

The three men were out of the door again, two of
them carrying another brazier and the third an armful
of weapons. The carriers put the brazier down and one
of them pointed at Uncle Chacha. The third man
dropped the weapons, lifted the trumpet and blew, just
as the ax crashed in again. One fierce note floated
across the green.

The knight heard it, looked over his shoulder, saw
the pointing arm, saw his attacker, and kicked the big
horse around. As it turned he hooked the ax back onto
his belt and lifted the lance out of its holder on the
return movement. The pennon dipped. The brazier
party stood still to watch the fun. The knight's boots
drubbed mercilessly at the horse's ribs, so that horse

and man rushed on Uncle Chacha like a landslide. Uncle Chacha glanced once over his shoulder to see whether danger threatened from behind, then waited for the charge, his curved gray blade held low in his right hand. Nicky tried to look away again, but the dread of the sight held her transfixed.

Uncle Chacha just stood and waited for the lance point. He was a round, easy, still target. Only when the bitter tip was a second away did he begin to move, to his left, out from the path of the horse.

Nicky gulped. He had dodged too soon. The point had followed him around.

But with a single flowing twist, long after he had seemed committed to his leftward dodge, he was rolling and falling to the right, in toward the battering hooves, the way the knight could not expect him to go; and then, as the spear point spiked uselessly past, he was still falling but rolling out, with his sword whistling up behind his back in a long, wristy slash.

The stroke did not seem to have hit anything, but by the time the knight was turning his horse for a fresh charge Uncle Chacha was on his feet and picking up something from the grass—a stick with a red rag near the end. Three foot of severed spear. He felt the point, turned for a moment to wave a cheerful hand to Nicky, threw his small round shield to one side and waited for the knight in the same pose as before—except that now the pennoned point hung parallel to the sword, his left hand grasping the cut shaft.

The three men by the stables had put the brazier down and were sharing out the weapons. One of them shouted to the knight and he called back, then came again more cautiously.

His boots drubbed and the horse bore in. The knight seemed to have an incredible advantage, fighting down at the small round man from that moving tower of muscle, and protected too by all his armor. And his ax— though he had to hold it one-handed, rather far up the shaft, as he needed his other hand for the reins—was so heavy that even held like that any blow from it would surely cleave turban and skull. The knight seemed to think so, for he was grinning as he came.

Uncle Chacha balanced to meet the charge. Nicky thought she knew what he would do. He would wait again until his enemy was almost on him, feint one way to commit the ax to a blow that side, then dodge around the other side of the horse and either pull the knight from his saddle, or wound or kill the horse so that he could fight the knight level. He would have to be quick, though: the other three men would soon be dangerously near.

But this time he didn't wait. When the horse was six feet away from him he made a long skip to his right, so that the knight had to turn the horse in to him, one-handed. As the big animal came awkwardly around,

Uncle Chacha moved again, leaping forward with a shrill, gargling shout. The knight's ax came up, ready for him, but the fat man leaped direct for the charging horse, sweeping the pennoned spear sideways and up in front of its nose at the very moment that the wolf-cry of his shout cut short in a snapping bark. The terrified horse, bred and trained to pull brewers' drays through orderly streets, shied sideways from the onslaught, and half reared in a swirling spasm that gave the knight far too much to do to allow him to smite at his attacker. Uncle Chacha struck with his sword and the knight had to drop the reins and raise his iron arm to parry the whistling blade; even before the steel clanged into the drainpipe, the knight's own spear point was lancing up into the armpit which the raised arm had exposed.

He was still grinning as he toppled.

Uncle Chacha, bouncy as a playful cat, flicked around the plunging animal and his blade flashed through the air again. Nicky heard the thudding jar of the iron doll hitting the turf, but no cry at all. Then the horse was careering off toward the woods and she could see how the knight lay, his feet toward her, his gold curls hidden by the bulk of his armored shoulders, and the half spear still sticking into him, straight up, as though it had been planted there to mark the place where he fell.

The men from the stables were only ten yards further off. Nicky yelled "Look out!" and pointed. Without pausing to study the danger Uncle Chacha lugged the spear from the carcass and ran for the barn. To fight more than one enemy you must have your back against a wall. Nicky left the window and rushed down the stairs, barely noticing as she crossed the loft that Ajeet now had the woodman's son locked in a death wrestle with a six-armed ogre. The children sat as still as if there'd been nothing outside the window but birdsong.

Gopal had been watching the duel through the long slit where the knight's two blows had knocked a whole plank out. Now he was lifting the bar of the door.

"Shut it behind me!" he hissed. "He cannot fight three men!"

"Wait!" whispered Nicky. "Then you might catch one of them from behind."

A thud told that Uncle Chacha had his back to the planking. Peering through the slit, Nicky saw the rush of his pursuers falter as he faced them—they had seen what had happened to the knight. They were all three terribly young, just murderous loutish boys, eighteen at the oldest. Now they quailed before the hard old warrior standing at bay, glanced uncertainly at each other and crept forward with their swords held stiff and low. They must have plundered some museum for them.

Gopal crouched where the doors joined, like a runner settling into his blocks at the start of a race. The robber at the near end passed out of Nicky's line of sight, his back toward her.

"Now!" she whispered, and threw her weight against

the big leaf. Gopal stayed in his crouch until the gap was wide enough; just at the moment when steel tinkled on steel outside, he exploded through. Nicky forgot her duty and rushed after him.

The nearest man had heard, or felt, the movement of the door and had half turned, so that the point of Gopal's sword drove into the soft part of his side below the rib cage. His face contorted; with a bubbling yell he buckled and collapsed. But the small blade had gone in so deep that his fall wrenched the hilt out of Gopal's hand, and the boy now stood weaponless.

The middle man, who had just skipped back out of reach of a lunge from Uncle Chacha's lance, wheeled at the cry, then rushed toward this easier victim. Gopal waited his coming hopelessly, but knowing that you have more chance if you can see your enemy than if you have your back to him. Nicky, who had checked her outward rush as the first man keeled over, scooped up some turf from the stack by the barn door and hurled it, two-handed, over Gopal's shoulder into the attacker's face. The brilliant summer had dried the turf into fine dust, barely held together by the dying roots of grass. The man staggered in his charge, blinded, and the next instant Uncle Chacha's lance had caught him full in the neck.

The third man dropped his sword and ran around the corner of the barn. No one chased him.

Without a word Nicky and Gopal walked panting to

the other side of the doors, where there were no corpses, and leaned against the wall. Uncle Chacha picked up his shield and joined them.

"Three more killed," he said, "and one run away. Not bad."

"What happened at the house?" said Gopal.

"They are good soldiers. Many of them slept with weapons by their beds. Wazir is dead, and Manhoor, and young Harpit. We have killed perhaps half of them, but a group are defending themselves in the big bedrooms on the far side. We are hunting through the other rooms before we attack them. Perhaps we will have to burn the house around them. Look."

A man, an Englishman, was running along the top of an eight-foot wall. He must have climbed from an upstairs window. Another figure, turbaned, dashed out of a door, planted its legs wide apart and raised its arms in an age-old pose. The arc of the risaldar's bow deepened; then it was straight. The man on the wall threw his arms wide between pace and pace and tumbled with a crash through a greenhouse roof.

"I must go back," said Uncle Chacha.

"I expect the other horses are in that stable," said Nicky, "and the rest of the armor. If you turned the horses out you could set fire to the stable and burn the saddles and things as well, and then you wouldn't have to fight any more knights on horseback."

"You are right," said Uncle Chacha, and trotted off

across the grass, still as light on his feet as if he hadn't spent the morning fighting for his life against grisly odds.

"You go too," said Nicky. "He'll need a hand with the brazier. I'm going to take the children home."

"That was a good throw, Nicky," said Gopal. "Thank you."

He gave her a gay salute with his bloody sword, made two practice slashes with it, and ran off after his uncle. Nicky climbed to the loft with legs like lead.

Ajeet's tiger was dead, with its skin nailed to the temple door. In the temple the woodman's sons were marrying queens.

Nicky nodded to Ajeet, who put her palms together under her chin.

"And so ends the tale of the tiger who had no soul," she said.

The children watched her in silence.

"Thank you, miss," said the redheaded girl.

"I'm going to take you all to your homes now," said Nicky.

A squealing like a piggery racked the loft.

"Quiet!" she yelled, and the squealing died.

"Now listen to me," said Nicky. "My friends have killed half the robbers. Ajeet's father beat the worst of the men on horses and killed him too. The rest of the robbers are shut up in the house, but a few have run away. Some of them may be hiding in the woods, but it's all right—they can't hurt us if you do what I say. There's a pile of flints by the ditch over there, and I want you each to pick up two of them, or three if you've got a pocket to put the third one in. Choose stones which are the heaviest ones you can throw properly and straight. Carry one in each hand, and if you see anybody who looks like a robber, lift up your arm and be ready to throw, but don't throw till I shout. Do you understand? Just think—thirty big stones, all held ready for throwing. One man won't attack an army like that. You're an army now. Soldiers. And you're going home."

She led them down the ladder. Ajeet came last. By the flint pile she marshaled them into a crocodile, with the smallest children in the middle clutching their useless but heartening pebbles. But the big boys and girls, back and front, were armed with flints that really would make an enemy hesitate. She looked for the last time toward the house. A flurry of shouts and a scream rose from the far side. A wisp of smoke came from the stable, and Gopal was leading a huge horse over the grass toward her.

"The other one bolted," he said, smiling. "But this one is too darn friendly. Can you take him with you?"

Nicky dithered, frightened by the animal's size.

"I'm used to horses, miss," said the redheaded girl. "I'll mind him."

She took the halter and Gopal started back toward

the battlefield, in a careful copy of Uncle Chacha's energy-preserving trot.

"Now," said Nicky, "I don't want to go past the house and along the road because that might make things difficult for my friends. Who knows the best way across the fields?"

Several voices answered and all the hands pointed the same way. She chose a dark, sensible-looking boy as her guide and set off. They crossed the big lawn, skirted a little wood, used a tarred footbridge to cross a dry ditch among bamboos, and came to a gate at the end of the garden. They wound slowly up the wheatfield beyond, tramping their path through stalks which had already dropped their seed and were now so brittle that the first gale of winter would push them over to lie and rot. A sudden rustling, as of a large animal disturbed, shook the stems to their left.

"Ready!" shouted Nicky. Thirty fists came up with rocks poised—though the pudgy arms at the center scarcely rose above the wheat stalks. Out of the wheat a naked man bounded like a startled deer. He gazed wild-eyed at the children for a moment; then, amid whoops and jeers, he was scampering up the hill. Nicky called her army into line of march again. That must have been the man she first saw escaping across the lawn in the gray, chill air before sunrise. She looked to her left and was astounded to see that the sun had still not crossed the low hilltop, though the air was gold with its coming. Less than an hour ago, then, the attack had begun.

Her guide led them slantwise up to a second gate, beyond which was a pasture full of cows who stared at them in stolid boredom as they trooped across. The cries from the house were faint and few now, but a strange mutter seemed to be growing in the village. The next gate led into a lane, all arched over with hazels, which her guide wanted to turn along; but Nicky thought they were still dangerously close to the big house and insisted on pushing through the fields behind the straggle of cottages that ran down the main road to the Borough.

More pasture here, and they had to skirt around a marshy piece where the stream that flowed through the White House gardens rose. The mutter from the village was like the roar of surf, and above it floated indistinguishable human shouts. Looking to her right as they slanted down toward the uproar, Nicky saw a slow column of smoke billowing up into the blissful morning. She realized what had happened.

"Run!" she cried. "Run, but keep together!"

If they didn't reach the road in time, a hundred maddened villagers would be roaring down to the big house to slaughter every living thing there, Sikh or robber. It was no use reaching the road alone—she had to come with all the children, safe. The villagers had seen the smoke from the stables and decided that the robbers had fired the barn where their hostages lay. And it would be the Sikhs' fault.

The line moved down hill, slowed to the pace of exhausted and ill-fed six-year-olds stumbling through the tussocks.

"You three," gasped Nicky to the older ones nearest her, "run to the road. Try to stop the village from attacking my friends. Tell them all the children are safe."

The messengers went down the slope in a happy freewheeling gallop, as if it had been a game for a summer evening. Nicky grabbed the wrists of the two smallest children and half helped, half hauled them over the hummocky turf. Other children dropped their flints and copied her. And here was a path, a narrow channel between the wall of a chapel and the fence of a pub garden, and now they were in the road, gasping, while the three messengers shrank from the roaring tide of the enraged village as it poured down the road toward them, led by little old Maxie waving a carpenter's hammer. The men were yelling, but the women were silent, and they were more terrible still: marching in their snowy aprons, faces drawn into gray lines with rage and weeping, fingers clenched around the handles of carving knives and cleavers.

Terrified by the sight, Nicky's army melted to the walls of the road. She stood helpless in the middle, still gripping the fat wrists of the two small children.

The tide of vengeance tried to halt, but the villagers at the back, who could not see what had happened, jostled into the ones who could. The news spread like flame through dry hay. The roaring anger changed and became a great hoarse splendor of cheering and relief. Mother after mother dropped her weapon and ran forward, arms outstretched. They came in a white whirl, like doves homing to the dovecote, and knelt in the road to hug their children.

Nicky ran to Maxie.

"Can you get the men to come and help my friends?" she cried. "They've killed half the robbers, but they're still fighting."

Maxie looked around at the bellowing crowd and nodded.

"Lift me up, Dave," he crowed to the stout man beside him.

Dave and another man swung him up to their shoulders as if he'd been a child held high to watch a king come past. He raised his arms like Moses on the mount and waited for the cheering to die.

"Men o' Felpham," he crowed. "You know as the Devil's Children have rescued our childer out of the hands of the robbers. Now they're fighting them to the death down at White House. Do we go help them?"

A mutter of doubt ran through the crowd.

"We've taken the horses," cried Nicky. "Look, I've brought one. And we've burned the place where the armor was, and we've killed half the robbers. We've killed the worst of the horsemen."

The mutter changed its note, and rose.

"Do we go help them?" crowed Maxie again. "Or do we let it be said that the men o' Felpham stood and watched while a handful of strangers did their fighting for them?"

The mutter returned to the note that Nicky had first heard, the noise of surf in a gale.

"Okay, Dave," said Maxie, "you can put me down."

The women pulled their children aside to let the bellowing army pass. Nicky picked up a fallen cleaver and walked beside Maxie.

"Five of my grandchilder there," he said. "You go home now, girl. This is no business for a child."

"I'm coming to make sure you don't hurt my friends," she said.

"Shan't do that. Not now."

"Well, I'm coming anyway."

Maxie looked over his shoulder.

"Hey!" he crowed. "You get off that horse, Dave Gracey, and let the girl ride. She'll be safer up there."

The stout man slid down, grinning, and whisked Nicky up to the broad and cushiony back. She had ridden ponies on holidays, sometimes, but never a creature as tall as this, never bareback and without reins, though Dave Gracey still held the halter. She seemed a mile in the air, and clutched the coarse mane with her left hand.

But after a minute she found that she wasn't afraid of the height, because the back was so broad and the horse's movement, at this pace, so steady, that she might have been riding on a palanquin. She let go of the mane, rested the cruel cleaver across her lap, straightened her back and neck and rode like a queen.

The exultation of victory thrilled through her blood. They had nearly done it now. All through the long night stalk, and the taut waiting, and the short blind blaze of action, she had felt nothing. She had simply thought and acted as the minute demanded. Even fear (and she had been horribly afraid) came from outside, pulsed through her, and was gone. But now she thought, "We have nearly done it." Glory washed over her like sunrise.

Now she knew why the robber knight had laughed like a lover as he clove at the tarred planks. The same glory was in him; but in him it had gone rancid.

It was a good half mile from the Borough to the White House. The village bellowed its coming all the way.

The besieged robbers must have heard them, realized that flight was the only hope now and made a desperate sortie. For as the village turned into the White House drive they met a dozen of their oppressors. Beyond, on the far side of a little bridge, came the weary Sikhs.

The village halted, faced by these armed and pitiless enemies. Another second and their courage might have oozed away as fast as it had risen; but Nicky kicked as hard as she could at the horse's sides, swung her cleaver up and shouted "Come on!"

The great beast trundled forward and the roaring rose behind her once again. A robber lunged at her with a short lance, but she saw the stroke coming and bashed the point aside with the flat of her cleaver. Another man fell as the horse simply breasted him over. The second rank of robbers turned to run back over the bridge. But there on the other side, swords ready, waited the grim Sikhs. The robbers hesitated, and the village churned over them.

Nicky was already among her friends. Gopal was there and Uncle Chacha and Kewal and the risaldar, weary as death but smiling welcome amid their beards. She dropped from the horse and ran to drag Maxie out of a ring of shouting and backslapping friends. He came without question.

"This is Mr. Maxie," she said. "This is Mr. Jagindar Singh."

The two men shook hands. Blood was still seeping from a crooked slash that ran from Uncle Jagindar's wrist to his elbow.

"I reckon we owe you a lot, sir," said Maxie. "More'n we can rightly pay."

"You will pay us well if we can now be friends," said Uncle Jagindar.

Chapter 8

FIVE STONES

Kaka and Gurdial and Parsan won the fancy-dress parade at the spring festival. Kaka was the back legs of the elephant, Gurdial was the front legs, and Parsan, aged two, dressed in brilliant silks and jewels, rode in the tiny howdah and was the princess. In fact the Sikh children, with their unfair advantage of looking slightly fancy-dress anyway, might have won every prize in the parade if the vicar hadn't been diplomatic enough to give the second prize to Sarah Pritchard, who came as a flaunting gypsy. She was Mr. Tom's great-niece.

On the other hand the village won the tug-of-war and (to the risaldar's disgust) the archery; and, of course, all the cake-making contests—there was no prize for chapati. But then Mr. Surbans Singh won the plowing match, cleaving a line so straight behind his big dray horse that you'd have thought he had a cord to steer by. Nicky didn't win anything, though she bowled and bowled for the pig. Kewal told her that if there'd been a disobedience prize, the dog which she'd found limping through the January snow on the common would have beaten any dog the village could put up. Kewal was wearing his gold turban and had spent all night with his beard in curlers; every girl in the village made eyes at him, and with his squint he had the advantage of being able to ogle two at a time. He strutted as though he'd won the battle against the robbers single-handed. (He had, in fact, been very brave but not—Uncle Chacha once hinted—very skillful, having neglected his sword practice.)

After the fancy dress parade was over and Kaka and Gurdial and Parsan had been given their prize—a white rabbit—the trumpet sounded for the main event of the festival. The trumpet was the one the robbers had used for their signals; before that it must have blown in a pop group; now it was half the village band.

The bowling for the pig stopped, and the women left off chaffering at the stalls and began to summon their children from their squealing chase among the elders' legs. Everybody trooped away, the young men down to the old cricket pavilion to collect their weapons, and the rest to line the Borough and the short street up to the churchyard. The old lady, Ajeet's grandmother, waited on her cart at the widest part of the Borough and Maxie stood on a crate beside her. Maxie was mayor now; the village hadn't fancied being ruled by another Master, so, soon after the battle, they had elected a mayor and councillors. Uncle Jagindar was a councillor.

Away to the right, from the cricket pavilion, the trumpet blew again. This time it was playing not a call but a tune, "The British Grenadiers," which was the only march the trumpeter could get the whole way through. A clumsy drum rattled in support. The village stood murmuring and craning, waiting for the soldiers to pass.

First marched the two standards. Kewal carried a gold lion embroidered on a black cloth, to symbolize the fact that "Singh" means "lion." The village had chosen, mysteriously, a sheep. (The vicar had liked that, and had preached a sermon on the text "The lion and the lamb shall lie down together.") The sheep was white, on a green cloth, and one of Mrs. Sallow's cousins carried it.

Next came the trumpet and the drum, and behind them the risaldar and the six bowmen from the village. If you knew the risaldar well you could see that beneath his proud bearing he was still sulking about the archery contest. Last of all came the infantry, fifty swords strong. Uncle Jagindar had hammered and tested every sword.

There was no cavalry, because all the village ponies were too busy hauling and plowing to be trained for warfare. The big dray horses which the robbers had brought hauled and plowed too: neither Sikhs nor villagers had thought it right that three men should ride proud while the rest walked.

The soldiers saluted the old lady and Mr. Maxie with their swords as they passed; they all looked as though they knew how to handle their weapons. Mr. Maxie waved an affable hand, as though he were saying good-bye to a visitor from his doorstep, and the old lady put her palms together and bowed with antique grace. The procession wheeled right, up toward the church, and the whole village and all the watching Sikhs crowded behind. Nicky and Ajeet and Kaka and Gurdial trundled the old lady's cart up the slope.

Mr. Tom's brilliant notion had solved the puzzling question of the monument. The three dead Sikhs were of course not Christians, and neither Sikh nor villager thought it proper that their monument should be in the churchyard. But two villagers had also died, one first of all and the other by a bitter fluke meeting a robber's sword in that last rush over the bridge. These two were Christians—at least since May. So five great stones had been found, and a stonemason had been brought over from Bradley to square them up and set them into the churchyard wall ("neither in nor out," as Mr. Tom had claimed). The mason had then cut a single name deep into each stone.

ARTHUR BARNARD

WAZIR SINGH

MANHOOR SINGH

HARPIT SINGH

DAVID GRACEY

Thousands of daffodils and a few hellebores and primroses stood in vases and jars along the top of the wall and in a thick mass on the ground below it.

The vicar, very nervous and breathy with emotion, preached a short sermon from the old mounting block beside the monument. Despite his donnish accent he managed to say what everybody felt was right, about how the two communities needed each other, both in peace and war. Uncle Jagindar read a brief prayer in Punjabi and then translated it into English, adding that words like "courage" and "love" meant the same thing in any language. Finally the trumpet played "God Save the Queen," just as if anybody knew what had happened to the Queen since May. Everyone cheered.

"Very English," whispered Kewal in Nicky's ear. She trod on his foot, on purpose.

The army dispersed and the weapons were put away, though many of the villagers now copied the Sikhs and

wore their swords wherever they went; the men relaxed
and chatted while the women got supper ready and the
village children taught the Sikh children how a maypole
worked and the bigger boys played football. Nicky noticed an odd group around the old lady's cart, Mr.
Maxie and Mr. Tom and Neena and Uncle Jagindar, all
talking earnestly. Quite often one of them would glance
across to where she sat against the pavilion wall fon-
dling her stray dog's ears.

It was a lucky night, warmer than usual for April,
under a dull sky. Stars would have been pretty but
would have meant frost, which no one wanted either for
sitting out in or for the sake of the vegetable patches
which were sown and showing. But even in that com-
parative mildness they were glad to sit within feel of the
huge bonfires which had been built at the bottom of the
recreation ground. The spit-roast mutton was very
good, and the home-baked bread much nicer than
chapati, Nicky decided.

After supper she didn't feel like joining in anything,
though there was dancing between the bonfires—whole
lines or circles of dancers moving in patterns with a
prancing motion which overcame the roughnesses of
the turf, while Mr. Tom's lion-headed fiddle sawed out
the six-hundred-year-old tunes. Ajeet had attracted a
ring of small children around her, a little beyond the
circle, and was telling them a story which made some of
them tumble about with laughter. Nicky sat and leaned

her back against the wheel of the old lady's cart and longed to be less stupid at Punjabi, so that she could talk to her without a translator. They were somehow the same kind of people, Nicky knew, herself and the old lady—hard, practical, wild, loving. But though Ajeet or Gopal gave her a long lesson every day, so that she could now understand quite a bit of the talk, she couldn't speak more than the easiest sentences back. She had never been any good at languages, not French, not German, and now not Punjabi.

So she leaned against the wheel and watched the pattern of dancers in the orange light of the bonfires, and the huge oval of faces, and the sudden fountain of curling sparks that erupted when a log collapsed. Neena came out of the dark and sat beside her.

"Are you happy, Nicky?"

"No, I don't think so. I don't know. I ought to be, but I'm not."

"What do you want?"

"I don't know that either."

"We've been talking about you."

"Yes, I noticed."

"We think it's time we tried to get you back to your own family."

"Please don't talk about it. Please!"

"No, listen, Nicky. Mr. Maxie's cousin is a sailor at Dover. Mr. Maxie sent a message to him and he heard the answer yesterday. Ever since . . . since all these changes happened, boats have been going over to France, ferrying people away. Millions of people have gone. And the French have set up offices all along the coast, where they take everybody's name very carefully. The French are good at that sort of thing. It may take a little while, but in the end they will find your parents for you, and all this will become just like a dream, or a story that Ajeet tells."

"But why should anyone take me to France? What can I do in exchange?"

"We will pay them."

"But no one's got any money, not anymore."

"The smallest of my mother's rings would buy a fishing boat ten times over. And she would give every jewel she owns to make you happy, Nicky. I sometimes think she loves you more than any of her own children or grandchildren. It is strange, is it not, how sometimes a soul will speak to a soul across language, across the generations, across every difference of race and birth and breeding."

Neena spoke some sentences of Punjabi. Nicky knew enough to understand that she was translating what she had just said. Nicky put up her hand and felt the other hand take it, felt the hard, cold knuckles and the harder rings.

"Mr. Maxie's cousin will come and fetch you next week," said Neena. "He will see you safely right out to the middle of the Channel, where the big ships wait and the madness ends. Mrs. Sallow insists that she will go with you as far as the sea, so that you are not among strangers."

"I don't want to go," said Nicky. "I daren't."

"But why? You have dared and adventured much more terrible things. This should not frighten you."

"It's not that kind of fright. It's . . . I don't want to explain."

Neena spoke quietly in Punjabi, and there was a short silence.

"Nick-ke," said the old voice above her head.

"Ai?" said Nicky.

The old lady began to speak, her voice dry and quiet, like the sound of a snake rustling across hot rocks in her own far country. This time it was she who spoke in short sentences, so that Neena could translate.

"Nicky, you are in danger. It is not the sort of danger we have fought through this last year. It is inside you. We have been in bad times. We have all had to be hard and fierce. But you have made yourself harder and fiercer than any of us, even than us Sikhs. In bad times you have to wear armor around your heart, but when times are better you must take it off. Or it becomes a prison for your soul. You grow to the shape of it, as a tortoise grows to the shape of its shell. Nicky, you must go to a place where you can take your armor off. That place is your parents' hearth."

Nicky felt a chill in her bones which was not the chill

of the night air. The small smithy under her ribs started its hammering, and in her mind's eye she saw the iron doll topple, grinning and jointless from his huge horse.

"How did you know about the armor?" she whispered.

Neena translated, and the old lady's cackling laugh surprised the night. Then the snake-rustling sentences began again.

"I was married when I was twelve. To a man I had never seen. It was the custom of our people. I loved my parents and my brothers and sisters and our happy house, and then I was taken away from them. I too put armor around my heart. But I was luckier than you, Nicky, for my husband—oh, how old he seemed—was kind and patient and clever. He made a place, a world, in which I wanted to take my armor off."

"Perhaps they're dead," said Nicky.

"Perhaps they are not. Perhaps you will not find them. Who can say? But until you have tried to find them you will make yourself stay hard and fierce. That is the danger of which I spoke. It is in your nature to become like that forever."

And that was true. Nicky knew that her kinship with the robber knight went deeper than the armor, deeper than the glorious wash of victory she had felt on the morning of the battle. Yes, she must go. But still she felt reluctant.

"Must I go so soon?" she said. "Next week is . . ."

"You must go now," said Neena decisively. "We have not talked to the village about this, but we think that all this island is closing in on itself. Soon they will have forgotten about how to get people away; they will have forgotten about France. We must expect difficult times."

"Then I ought to stay and help you," said Nicky obstinately.

"No. We have learned to be careful. We will survive and prosper. If you ever come back, you will probably find that Jagindar is an earl. Nicky, you don't have to go. We all love you here, and we should like you to stay, out of our own selfishness. But we think you should try to go to your family."

Nicky made up her mind, as usual, in one irrevocable rush.

"Yes," she said. "Yes, I will go. But perhaps one of you could come with me as far as the sea. Kewal or Uncle Chacha or Mr. Surbans Singh."

Neena sighed in the dark, and Nicky could hear the rustle of her sari as her shoulders made the familiar shrug.

"It would be nice, Nicky, but it would not be safe. Outside these few fields we are still the Devil's Children."

And After . . .

Nicky was lucky. She bought a passage on an almost empty fishing boat. In mid-Channel they hove to beside a large steamer and she climbed aboard, only finding it strange that she did not find it strange. At Calais the refugee agencies searched their files and sent her to a camp where she found her parents waiting in the long queue, as they'd done every day for many months. Despite the drabness of the huts, finding them was like coming out of an icy, drizzling street into a warm house full of friendship.

Nicky's ship was one of the last few to leave. Britain, as Neena had foreseen, closed in on itself, like an anemone in a rock pool closing at a touch. When other nations tried to probe into the island, the island seemed to grow a mysterious wall around it. It was very difficult to get even a single spy through.

But behind the wall we began to change. The Changes were mostly inside us, in our minds, but a few were outside. In a bare hill valley a great oakwood grew, overnight, with a tower in the middle of it. In Surrey that wild Dervish who had caused the panic when Nicky lost her parents discovered that the thunderstorm had been no accident. He had willed it into being, and now he could will any weather he chose. He didn't know how, nor did the others (a boy in Weymouth, a schoolmaster in Norwich, for instance) who found they had the same gift. In a year or two it was just a commonplace that there would be sun for harvest and snow in December, accepted by everyone in much the same way that they accepted that a chestnut tree would grow its five-fingered leaves every spring.

But not everyone was aware of the weathermongers at work, because not every district had its own weathermonger, and just as the island closed in on itself, so the cells inside it also closed. Men lived by rumor. Events in the next county became strange and far away. One winter, for instance, it was said in Yorkshire that dragons had begun to stir in the Pennine hills; quite sensible farmers took to sleeping with buckets of water beside their beds, ready to quench the fiery breath.

Most of the customs that grew up were concerned with witch-craft (as the use of machines was called). These also varied from shire to shire. Hereford, for instance, was very little troubled by witches and the reason for this (men believed) was the great Hereford Flower Dance, which lasted for fourteen days in May and was a time of singing and happiness, a celebration of the power of Nature against the horror of engines.

By contrast there were the great witch-findings in Durham Cathedral, with three thousand people massed under the frowning Norman arches, pale-cheeked and sweating, groaning all together as name after name was called, neighbors and wives and sons and cronies, to stand the unappealable tests.

All these things flowed from the Power that had been woken beyond the stone slab. In such an island, so secretive, so unpredictable, how could a spy from the outside world survive? That is another story.

About the Author

PETER DICKINSON is an award-winning writer whose books include, in addition to The Changes Trilogy, *City of Gold* (winner of the Carnegie Medal), *Tulku* (winner of the Carnegie Medal and the Whitbread Award), *The Blue Hawk* (winner of the Guardian Award), and *Chance, Luck, and Destiny* (winner of the Horn Book Award for nonfiction). His most recent book for Delacorte Press was *Healer* (a *School Library Journal* Best Book). Mr. Dickinson lives in England.